The Hunt
for the
Se7enth

MICHAEL
LOCKE'S
BOOK

MICHAEL LOCKE'S BOOK

The Hunt for the Seventh

Christine Morton-Shaw

SCHOLASTIC INC.
New York Toronto London Auckland
Sydney Mexico City New Delhi Hong Kong

ISBN-13: 978-0-545-20679-2
ISBN-10: 0-545-20679-0

12 11 10 9 8 7 6 5 4 3 2 1   9 10 11 12 13 14/0

Printed in the U.S.A.   40

First Scholastic printing, October 2009

Typography by Larissa Lawrynenko

This one is for Greg, Nathan, and Robin

The Ghost in Man, the Ghost that once was Man,
But cannot wholly free itself from Man,
Are calling to each other thro' a dawn
Stranger than earth has ever seen; the veil
Is rending, and the Voices of the day
Are heard across the Voices of the dark.

—TENNYSON

to village ↵ | river

to parking lots ←

woodlands

ancient

ruined
chapel

rhododendrons

lavender   beds

underground path of overflow →

Bartholomew's

stone
weir

ex

Minerva

L

old stable blocks

copse

Topiary
Garden

monks' walk

island

Wildflower
Gardens

maze

Topiary
Garden

arbor

ancient

vines

Italian
Garden

Rose
Garden

woodlands

troughs

icehouse

apple and
pear orchard

kitchen an
garde

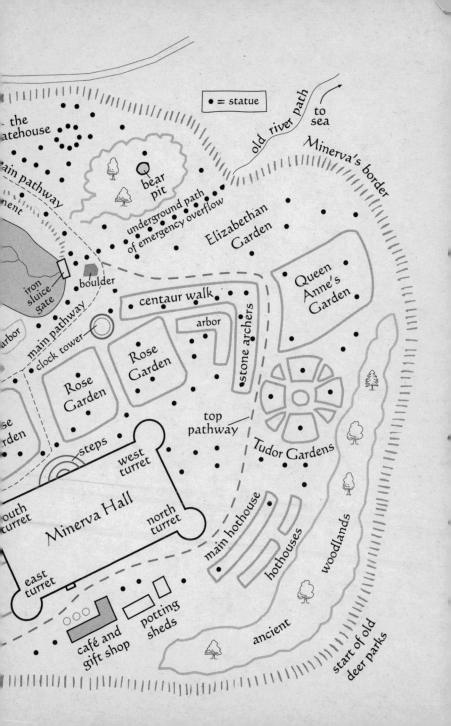

● = statue

... the
...atehouse

...ain pathway

...ent

old river path

to
sea

Minerva's border

bear
pit

underground path
of emergency overflow

Elizabethan
Garden

Queen
Anne's
Garden

iron
sluice
gate

boulder

...arbor

main pathway

centaur walk

clock tower

arbor

stone archers

top
pathway

Rose
Garden

Rose
Garden

...se
...rden

steps

west
turret

Tudor Gardens

Minerva Hall

north
turret

main hothouse

hothouses

woodlands

...uth
...turret

east
turret

café and
gift shop

potting
sheds

ancient

start of old
deer parks

PROLOGUE

S OMEBODY DIED HERE ONCE. I'm convinced of it. Somewhere here, in this huge garden. I feel them watching me.

It happens at odd times when I'm feeding the peacocks or helping Dad burn the fallen leaves. The back of my neck will prickle. My hands will go sweaty. *Turn around slowly,* I'll think. *There is someone behind me.* But when I turn around, there is never anyone there.

I can't tell Sal: she'd just get hysterical. Then I'd get into trouble for trying to scare my little sister again. And I can't tell Dad. He'd only think it was Mom. He'd get ill again; he'd sit like a stone for hours; he'd stop shaving, stop eating again. He'd lose this new job.

Me? Above all, I'd love it to be Mom. I'd give anything to be able to look up and see her there just one more time. But it's not Mom. She would never want to scare me.

It's a child, I think, because they seem to like playing games. They take me by surprise by rearranging the flowerpots or setting the swing swaying under the apple tree. But that's happened only twice. Most of the time they just creep up behind me. They move up very close. I can hear their breathing, sometimes even feel it on my neck.

The first time it happened was when the old gardener, Harold, was showing Dad around that very first day. It was windy, and they were struggling to keep the maps from flapping away across the lawns. We were in the Tudor Garden. Sal was skipping her way down the paths.

I was standing behind a cherub fountain, when suddenly I heard it. A breath; a soft footstep came up close behind me.

I peered out from behind the statue. I walked all around it twice. I was alone.

Yet I heard someone speak. It sounded like a young girl's voice—such a small, cold whisper.

"Find the Seventh!" she said.

Then the old gardener laughed at something Dad had said, and they strode off, maps flapping in their hands like struggling birds.

Find the Seventh.

I've described it all, except for the fear. The instant dry mouth. The sweat that forms. The tears that prickle. The sickly feeling.

Whoever it is who is watching me in the garden I'd rather not find at all.

But I can't tell Sal or Dad.

I don't know what to do.

CHAPTER ONE

WE'VE BEEN GIVEN some rooms all the way at the top of the south turret. They are the old embroidery rooms and the seamstresses' quarters from centuries ago. The retiring gardener showed us up some old back stairs that led from the kitchen. Then we came to a small landing with several doors leading off. One of these led to a narrow spiral staircase. We struggled up it with the suitcases.

"Always *always* use the back stairs," said the old gardener. "The master hates to meet up with anyone. Phew! Nearly there."

We came out into a long circular corridor with doors lining it. One by one he opened them, and we followed him into each curved room.

I've never lived in a turret before. I'll feel like a medieval knight! First, the bedrooms. The biggest one is for Dad. Mine and Sal's are crummy, small things, both leading off the living room. Sal instantly claimed the best one for herself. In my room there was nothing much except for a wonky bookshelf, filled with dusty old encyclopedias. One of them was being used to prop up one leg of a wobbly chair. The whole thing didn't look very promising. On the living room floor was a cat dish with some old tuna caked in it.

"Suki's vanished," Harold said. "Sulking, no doubt! She hates change. If she shows up, I've left my phone number on the kitchen bulletin board."

Sally looked around with her nose screwed up. "It's kind of . . . *smelly*!" she said. (At ten she is much too fussy about Everything.)

Next, we filed into a tiny kitchen and then a bathroom, with a dripping shower over an ancient bathtub. Then back to the chilly living room. And two tiny storerooms. Back in the curved corridor Dad sat down on a suitcase.

"It'll do," he said.

There was one door left unopened. I stared at it. "What's through there?" I asked.

Harold glanced at it briefly. "Through there? Nothing."

"How can there be nothing? It's a door!"

"It's locked," said Harold, as if that settled it. "I've never bothered with it myself."

But I didn't quite like the way he said it, as if he didn't

6

want to be asked any awkward questions. "Well, who has the key?" I insisted.

Harold frowned down at me. "If there's one thing the master dislikes more than children, it's questions! You'll find out when you meet him later." He nodded darkly to Dad. "And you two, you'd best keep your mouths shut around him, that's for sure."

I opened my mouth again, but Dad cut me short. "That's enough, Jim!" said Dad. "Let it go now."

He looked tired. Gray. So I let it go.

But it didn't let me go.

"Find the Seventh!" a young girl's voice whispered, right at my ear.

I glanced back at the door before scuttling to catch up with Dad in the living room. I was too scared to be out here by myself, even for a few seconds.

I wasn't sure I was going to like it here at all.

It was almost bedtime by the time we were finally summoned to the master's study. The royal summons. We walked nervously through the Grand Hall, upstairs, and along the echoing corridors. The passages were lit by dim lamps or, in more remote places, just the tiny glow of emergency lights set into the ceilings.

The only sounds were the ticking of the many clocks we

passed. Every so often as we walked along, I heard the faint whirring of something small, set high into the walls. This puzzled me until I glanced back and spotted the small electric red dot of a security camera as it swiveled our way.

I wondered who was watching us.

The butler met us at the top of a long flight of stairs. With an impassive face, he ushered us into a dim study and closed the doors on us. Now we were alone, just us and Lord Louis Minerva III.

He was sitting in his wheelchair in front of a huge log fire—a grumpy-looking old man with a glass of amber brandy in one hand. He gestured us to step forward into his golden halo of firelight. When he smiled at us, his eyes were cold and filled with dislike. He made me think of a lizard.

"Mr. Brown—and your delightful children! Do come in. I trust your rooms are sufficient?"

"Perfectly, thank you, sir," said Dad.

I glanced around the room. One whole wall held screen after screen, the monitors of a vast closed-circuit TV system. Each screen flickered with ghostly images of various parts of the grounds. There was the great staircase. And the calm face of the lake. And the gatehouse with its flag, floodlit, on top.

The only light came from the flickering fire and those screens flashing a cold silver from frame to frame. I began to feel as if I'd stepped into some old silent movie.

Lord Minerva gestured Sal and me to step even closer. He regarded us silently. This made both of us fidget. Eventually he gestured toward the screens.

"I don't get out much these days," he said with a tight little smile. "Nevertheless, as you can see, I am in complete control of my entire estate. I have eyes everywhere, some of them hidden. I trust I shall not have cause to regret your coming here."

He was staring more at me than at Sal. I got the impression there was something about me he didn't like at all.

"No doubt you will want to explore your new home," he said. "But may I remind you that this is my home, not yours. *Your* home, for now, is in the rooms at the top of the south turret. As for *my* home, there are only certain areas that are open to the public. The rest of Minerva Hall is roped off. You are forbidden to go beyond those boundaries. Do I make myself clear?"

"Yes, sir," I said. Sal nodded and stared down at the carpet. I could feel her begin to tremble slightly by my side.

I didn't blame her. He was a scary man. His face was filled with dislike. His eyes were dark, sharp, and piercing. Sal swallowed hard.

Dad, for once, picked up our unease. He stepped forward.

"My children's names are James and Sally," he said. "I think you'll find, sir, that they won't go anywhere they shouldn't."

I nudged Sal. We'd heard it, the clipped, polite way Dad

9

talks to people he *really* does not like.

"James and Sally, eh?" Lord Minerva observed. There was something slightly mocking in the way he said our names. He seemed to hate us already. "Well, James and Sally, take a good look at these closed-circuit TV screens there. Your father comes here on a trial basis. It would be a pity if you two were to mess things up for him—especially after his recent bereavement."

I felt my face going red. I hated the way he mentioned Mom like that . . . so coldly. I hated him. We glared at each other, he and I, until he turned his mean little eyes away at last.

"And now, Brown, if you would be so kind as to ring for Montague? Just pull that bellpull there. He will escort you back to the main staircase."

Dad pulled the embroidered bellpull beside the fire. The door opened instantly, and the butler came in. I got the distinct impression he had been listening at the door.

"If you would please follow me?" said he, very crisp and polite.

We filed out after him, strangely unsettled.

That night I lay awake, too scared to sleep.

It wasn't just the whispers I'd already heard. It was the feeling of such a massive, ancient house creaking all about me, the many dimly heard clocks chiming the night away. It was spooky, to say the least.

When Dad first told us he was going to be the Head Gardener at Minerva Hall, I'd never imagined a place as big as this. It's almost a castle, with four turrets and thousands of mullioned windows. There are sixty-two main rooms, apparently, and Good Queen Anne once came and slept her fat body in one of them. So people come and stare pointlessly at the enormous royal bed and then traipse around certain sections of the Hall.

At last on that first night I sat up in bed. It was hot and stuffy, so I went to the window and struggled to pull it open. The grounds were lit by floodlights here and there. I could just make out the dozens of white tourist signposts, which I knew pointed to the Tudor Garden or to the Elizabethan Gardens or to the great hothouses.

I let my eyes roam to the distant lake. Its face was quiet and calm. There was a tiny island in the middle of it, I noticed, filled with small trees. I wondered if there might possibly be a rowboat I could use. I made up my mind to try to explore the island, whether the master disapproved or not.

An owl hooted far away as I continued looking at it all. Nearer the house I could see the dark corner of the kitchen garden with all its hundreds of herb pots. There were the orchards, where the cook got fruits to make her famous chutneys and jams, to be sold in the gift shop.

The moon suddenly came out from behind the clouds and

lit up the strange shapes of the Topiary Garden, its hedges trimmed into the forms of castles or chessmen or cockerels. There was a bear pit somewhere too, I suddenly remembered, a real bear pit, where a real bear used to be chained up during Victorian days. And somewhere there was an enormous maze that people could get lost in for hours and hours.

And there were statues, statues everywhere. The old man loved his statues. Everywhere I looked there was another! They gave me the creeps, standing there so white and silent all over the estate.

Of course, I'd seen some of these already as we'd explored. Sal and I had tried to count them all, but we lost count after 103. There were statues of haughty queens and marbled giants who glowered over high hedges. Turning a corner of the Rose Garden, we came across groups of centaurs and archers, their muscles rippling. In one spooky section leading to the lake we'd found a row of hooded men who looked like monks. Their carved sandaled feet seemed to follow one another down the gravel paths soundlessly, their hands clasped in prayer.

My eyes traveled outward to the far edge of the estate. Somewhere in those dark trees stood a small family chapel. Harold had warned us about it. "*No one* is allowed in there. It's private," he'd said. "Don't go anywhere near it. And don't go getting in Cook's way, either."

That's another thing: People don't seem to use names here.

Just their occupations. "Cook" is really named Mrs. Benson. But everyone just calls her Cook. It's the same with them all.

Cook.

Second Cook.

Head Housemaid.

Master's Personal Butler.

Head Chambermaid.

The list goes on and on. Then there's a whole gaggle of Parlormaids.

But there's only one Head Gardener. That's Dad. He has a few undergardeners to help him, but they're only part-timers, so he's already worried that all this will be way too much for one man to do. Then, of course, there's Head Gardener's Boy. (That's me. Sal doesn't even get a title. There's no such thing as Head Gardener's Girl.)

I'm the only boy here. Well, so they *said*. But I know they were lying. There is definitely another boy here. Just after supper, when I went out to feed the peacocks, I spotted him sneaking into the maze.

It was dusk. The last of the tourists had just gone; the huge gates had swung closed for the night.

He looked a bit younger than me. Ten, eleven maybe? He wore a scruffy red fleece and dirty jeans. He was small and walked in a funny, plodding way, lifting his feet up too high. It was as if he were treading in glue and didn't want his feet to

13

get stuck. I called out to him, but he totally ignored me. I know he heard me, though, because he glanced around, then slunk into the maze anyway.

I decided I might go there the next night, go right into the maze and lie in wait, in case he came again. I would hide in the middle and jump out at him when he arrived. That would serve him right for ignoring me!

On that first night, as I stared over the grounds from my chilly turret window, something caught my eye. It was a small movement, a shadow, over there by the lake.

The moon went behind a cloud, and all I could see was what looked like a small, bent figure in black. But when the clouds moved on, it was gone. Something about this made me feel uneasy, unsafe.

Was there someone out there, creeping about? What was he doing? Was it the boy? Or someone else?

I thought again of that cold, urgent whisper I'd heard in the corridor, from someone I couldn't see.

"Find the Seventh!"

The Seventh what?

As I climbed back into bed, I found I was shaking. The whispered words wouldn't leave me. The cold whisper kept running around and around my head. Had I really heard it? I knew that I had. I just couldn't make sense of it.

It goes without saying that it was a long, long night.

CHAPTER TWO

T HE NEXT MORNING I heard the missing cat. It was meowing sadly, over and over. The sound was coming from the
locked room.

It must be Harold's cat! She must have gotten fed up with
sulking and was looking for him in his old rooms.

"Me, me, me!" cried the cat, over and over.

I put my eye to the keyhole. There was nothing but a faint
gloom. The thought of her starving to death in there was horrible.

I turned and ran to find Dad, down the spiral stairs, down
and down in that great house with shadows and windows
flashing past. I ran into the kitchen, where Dad was kneeling,
fiddling with something in the corner.

"Dad!" I panted. "I've found Suki, Harold's cat! She's
meowing like mad!"

The cook was there. She looked up from the stove, where the spout of the huge kettle gave off gentle wisps of steam.

"Dad, come *on*! We have to let her *out*; she's in the locked room—she'll be starving. Mrs. Benson, have you got any tuna?"

Mrs. Benson just shook her head, staring at me. "You heard a cat?" she said. "In the locked room?"

Why on earth was she looking at me like that? Meanwhile, Dad turned to face me. "Found Suki?" he said. "I don't think so, Jim. Look!"

By his side was an old cat basket he'd just finished tying with rope. Inside was a black cat, settling down onto a blanket.

"Meet Suki," said Dad. "The butcher found her when he delivered the weekly meat. She was stuck in the cold store. She's a bit chilly but hardly starving. She's as fat as a pig!"

She lay there, a smug thief, purring. Mrs. Benson poured hot water into a mop bucket.

"That cat always was greedy," she said. "I'll have to scrub the whole place down with disinfectant. Filthy animal! Sausages and chops scattered all over the place, and I can't begin to tell you what she did on the *floor*!"

She clattered off indignantly with a mop, along the passageway and into the cold store. I followed her in.

It was a freezing marble-lined room, the sort of meat locker they used to use before they had refrigerators. I could see my breath. Any meat in here would keep for the entire week. I

16

stood in the doorway and held my nose. If cats had public toilets, this is what one would smell like.

"Go away, child!" snapped Mrs. Benson. "You'll only step in something and trail it all the way through the house."

As I walked slowly back up all those stairs, I was still shivering.

Behind the locked door all was silent. I knelt and put my eye to the keyhole. Just then a new sound came: the unmistakable sound of footsteps.

Slowly they went from left to right, just behind the door. Then I heard them return. As they passed the door, the light was momentarily blocked.

The hair stood up all along my arms and neck.

Through the keyhole I caught a glimpse of white fur held in something blue. It was just a glimpse of something, quickly seen. A blue silken sleeve, a glimmer of lace, the pale flash of a child's hand.

The footsteps faded away. Spooked out, I ran to my room.

The white cat was not Suki. This cat had been held in someone's arms. And that someone was still in there, pacing.

And whoever it was, locked doors were no barrier to them at all.

The rest of that second day at Minerva Hall dragged by in boring hours of dust and unpacking and doing a million jobs to get ourselves organized. Sal and I bickered a lot. Just before supper I kept yawning so loudly that Dad snapped at me in the end. "For heaven's sakes, Jim! Get outside and get some fresh air! Here, take these out; go and find a Dumpster."

He shoved two garbage bags my way, both stuffed with crumpled newspaper packing.

"Can I come too?" Sal instantly asked me. "I'll carry one of the bags."

"No!" was my automatic reply. "You'll only slow me down."

"I will not! You've been in a horrible mood all day long," said Sal. "Hasn't he, Dad?"

I raced away before Dad made me take her and ran down the turret stairs three at a time. It was good to get outside, and anyway, I wanted to go to the maze and see if that boy was there again. I dumped the trash bags, then ran through the darkening gardens to the maze.

The hedges of this maze were really tall. No one could see over them once they were inside, not even if they jumped up high. That's why Dad needed a map; he was the one who had to trim all those hedges. "How would I ever get *out* again?" he'd muttered. "As if I'm not going to be busy enough, without spending hours lost in that thing!"

Now I had the map in my hands; I'd snatched it from Dad's coat pocket. I stopped at the entrance and looked all around.

It was a warm evening. Birds called to one another. There

was no sign of the boy. I peered at the map and entered the maze.

Right. Right. Left.

Straight ahead. Second left. First right.

Once I was in the maze, everything changed. It was like entering a computer game where all the walls were green. Every turn was green. The floor was green grass. I counted, turned, made a mistake, backtracked. Pretty soon I was an emerald green alien entering a strange green environment in which I had to zap anything that moved before it zapped me.

But no one told the midges that! They bit me half to death, and the farther I walked, the sweatier I became, and so they swarmed all the more. I kept breathing them in and having to spit them out again.

It was also rapidly getting dark, and I hadn't thought to bring my flashlight. The map was getting hard to see. I imagined myself in here till breakfast time tomorrow, never getting any nearer the center.

Suddenly I was there. There were no more twists and turns. There was just a white paved area with a circular bench on it and the usual statue in the middle.

So much for my taking the boy by surprise. He was already there, sitting on the bench!

I noticed again his grubby jeans and fleece. His very blond hair had an uncared-for look, too long and tangled. He wore brown boots with the wrong colored laces, bright blue. He had a piece of blue chalk in one hand.

He didn't even look up at me. He just sat with his head to one side as if listening hard. This threw me for a while. I folded up the map, wiped my sweaty hands, fidgeted.

"Hello," I said at last. "I *knew* there was another boy here! Apart from me, I mean."

He still didn't look at me. But he did speak.

"Six," he said.

"What?"

"Six children there are here. Apart from you, your sister, and *this* one." When he said "*this* one," he pointed to himself.

"Six other kids? Here? So where are they all then?" I looked around as if expecting all six to burst out at me at any minute.

"Six and two, it makes eight," he replied. "Eight, it is the largest cube number in the Fibonacci sequence. Nine it is, with the sister. Nine players there are on a baseball team. Cats, they have nine lives."

What was he talking about? What a strange way of talking he had. He was weird. He stared down at my shoes.

"The date of your birth, it was what?" he unexpectedly asked my shoes.

"Er, September," I said.

"The *numbers* of your birth date, they are what?"

"Er, the nineteenth of September, 1990."

20

"Wednesday's child." He nodded. "Full of woe."

"Wednesday's child?"

He began to recite part of a rhyme I vaguely remember Mom reciting too:

> *"Monday's child is fair of face.*
> *Tuesday's child is full of grace.*
> *Wednesday's child is full of woe. . . ."*

He chalked my date of birth on the white paving stone, as a number: "9-19-1990."

His grubby finger pointed to it. "This date number, it is a Wednesday. The year 1990, it is an interesting number on its own. It is a stella octangula number."

A what? I was lost. And as for my being born on a Wednesday—that was more than I knew! The kid was *seriously* weird. He stood up and walked quickly out of sight, around the corner of the nearest hedge.

Was he going? Just like that?

But no, he was still there. His voice called to me through the leaves.

"A map, it is never needed inside any maze," he said. "A person, he just has to follow the left-hand wall at all times and he will get in and he will get out again."

"Really?" I replied. "Wait! I'm Jim. What's your name?"

"They are coming now, and so this person will leave."

21

"Who's coming?" I asked.

But he left at a run. I heard his footsteps twist and turn, then fade away.

I sat down on the bench, dumbfounded. Not once in my life have I had a conversation with anyone who never looked at my face. And I still didn't know his name.

I decided to call him Einstein.

The sky was almost dark now. The map was next to useless. But my trusty Einstein had told me how to get out anyway. "Follow the left-hand wall," he'd said. So I went to the hedge and reached my hand out to the left-hand side and set off. At each turn, I just kept following the hedge that was still under my hand, brushing my fingers as I walked along.

I hadn't gone far when I heard footsteps on the other side of the hedge. They were walking in the same direction as I was, just on the other side. When I turned, they turned with me.

I smiled. So . . . Einstein had sneaked back. He was still in here, following me. Probably he was counting my footsteps and dividing the sum of them by the number of midges still buzzing around.

"That you, Einstein?" I called.

No answer. I stopped walking. So did he.

I started walking again. So did he.

"Okay," I shouted, "I know you're there! Play your little game!"

I ran a few paces. He ran a few paces. I slowed down. So did he.

My hand got sore from the spiky bits of hedge slapping against it. Turn, walk on, turn, walk on. I just kept going with Einstein's theory of maze escape. It was working. But he started to annoy me, ignoring me like this. How could I get him talking again?

Numbers. He obviously loved numbers. And dates.

"Hey, Einstein!" I called through the hedge. "When were *you* born?"

No reply. I tried again.

"Come on, brains, your turn now. What's *your* date of birth?"

Ahead of me a faint light gleamed. It was the light of the house, just reaching me. I must be very near the entrance.

I was. It had worked! This was the very last length of hedge. I walked along a bit more quickly. Einstein's footsteps hurried to keep up.

Five more steps to go. I could hear him, keeping pace on the other side of the hedge.

"Come on, Einstein!" I teased him. "What is your date of birth? And what's your *name*? I can't keep calling you Einstein, can I?"

Three steps. Two. One. I was out.

The footsteps also stopped.

Far away, across the lawn, I spotted that strange, plodding gait of Einstein as he walked away. Then I heard a young girl's voice, right in my ear. I whirled around, and my hair stood on end.

The faint image of a girl stood there. She was there, yet she was all gray and see-through. I could just make out long ringlets in her hair and a dress with huge, bunchy sleeves.

"My name is Harriet," she whispered. "And I was born in the year eighteen hundred and fourteen."

I backed away, my mind racing. Then she was gone.

Someone grabbed me—I almost jumped out of my skin— and Sal was there, tugging at my arm. "Jim, what on earth is the matter? You're all white. Dad said it's time for supper. What's wrong?"

"Er, nothing. Nothing's wrong."

"Well then, stop standing there and hurry up and come back in. I'm starving!"

Shaken, I followed Sally to the main kitchen.

We found Mrs. Benson loading two plates of toast onto a small wooden tray set into a square gap in the wall. The gap had small sliding doors, one on either side. These were open to show the tray. Mrs. B. heard us coming in and straightened up.

"Well, well!" she said. "Two hungry children! Lucky for you I haven't sent it up yet."

"Sent it up?" asked Sal.

She tapped the edge of the tray. "This unhygienic thing is called a dumbwaiter," she said. "It works on a winch system that sends the tray up through the house and into your living room."

"Why?" asked Sal instantly.

"Well, it certainly saves our legs! But in olden days this winch was used to send cloths and stuff up to the sewing rooms. Also, meals were sent up on it. See that handle?"

We nodded.

"Well, I was just about to crank your supper upstairs, but you've saved me the trouble. The crank gets hard to work after a while. Anyway, come and sit yourselves down."

We sat at the huge table, and Sal began eating the toast hungrily. I still felt all shaky. I sipped at the tea and watched Mrs. Benson fuss about, putting huge trays of sausage rolls into the enormous ovens. I toyed with my piece of toast.

"Not hungry, boy?" she suddenly said. "It's James, isn't it?"

"Jim. And this is Sal," I said.

"Sal, is it?" said Mrs. Benson. "Well, maybe Sal should get her braid out of the sugar bowl—if she wouldn't *mind*, that is!"

Sal snatched up her stray braid and began to suck sugar off the end. "Sorry," she muttered through her hair. She grabbed more toast.

Mrs. Benson reached over and pulled one hair out of the

sugar bowl. She held it between two fingers as if it were an insect, then dropped it into the garbage can. The entire contents of the sugar bowl followed it.

Sal and I exchanged glances as the sugar bowl was refilled. It was clear that Mrs. Benson was very particular about hygiene. She could also tell I was upset about something. She kept looking sideways at me. I didn't want her asking any awkward questions, so I racked my brains for something to say.

"Mrs. Benson?"

She replaced the full sugar bowl on the table—far away from Sally's braids.

"Well?" she said.

"Where were the Minerva family buried? Like . . . the children, the ones who lived here, I mean. Are their graves in that village we drove through?"

"Not there. There's a family graveyard here in the grounds. But I wouldn't try to find it if I was you. The master wouldn't like it. There were several children buried there, I believe. It was all very sad. They were hard days, way back then."

She sighed and began scrubbing a huge pan in the sink.

"Why sad?" I asked. "What happened to them?"

"One way or another, it's been an unlucky sort of family," she said. "Some say this whole valley is unlucky, but—oh, heavens, I do wish the kitchen girls would leave the pans to *soak*!"

26

I interrupted her grumbling. "How long have you lived here?"

Mrs. B. laughed. "Me? Live here? In *this* damp place? My poor bones wouldn't stand it—not with my arthritis! No, I come in from Sevenstone every morning. It's a fair ways up that hill too, especially in the snow."

The pan was being scrubbed to within an inch of its life. She peered inside it, spotted a minute speck of grease, and began to scrub it all over again.

"So how would I find out about the children of the family?" I persisted.

She rinsed the pan under the tap and raised her voice to be heard over the splashing. "Look, I'm busy here, and I've still got tomorrow's bread to do. If you need to find out anything about Minerva Hall, why not go on the guided tour? There's eight of them every day. You can ask away to your heart's content. The first one starts at nine in the morning."

"Starts where?"

"Main hall. At the foot of the grand staircase. And now, off you go. I don't mind you having your supper in here every once in a while. Henry sometimes does too, when he's home from school. But I can't have you hanging around for long."

"Henry?" asked Sal. The toast plate was empty.

Mrs. B. nodded. "Henry, the master's son," she said.

"That ancient old man has a *son*?" asked Sal incredulously.

27

Mrs. B. glanced at her, and her lips twitched slightly.

"The master married late," she replied. "But yes, he has a son. You just missed meeting him, actually; he left only a week ago. The master drove him back last Monday."

"Back where?"

"Back to his boarding school. It's a special school. Henry has a few—well, a few problems. A few strange ways."

"Like what?" asked Sal, subtle as ever.

"Well, Henry is autistic. He doesn't see life like we do. Loud noises scare him, for instance. He doesn't talk much. But he's a great boy all the same. Anyway, you can meet him when he comes back. Now, shoo!"

She flapped her dish towel at us as if we were flies.

All the way up the turret stairs, I was wondering about Henry. I didn't really know what *autistic* meant, but it was clear that Einstein had some very strange ways about him, that was for sure. So . . . was Einstein in fact Lord Henry? But if so, how come he was still here if he was supposed to have returned to school several days ago? It didn't make sense.

"Jim? Should we?" said Sal as she hurled herself onto the living room sofa.

"Should we what?"

"Do the guided tour tomorrow morning? We might as well," she went on. "There's not a lot else to do."

I hesitated. I hadn't really counted on Sal coming with me.

She started to unbraid her hair and continued speaking. "You never know—it might even be interesting!"

"Oh, yeah," I replied, trying to put her off. "Sure it will! It'll just be lots of boring facts and figures, just stupid adult stuff. Can't wait!"

"Don't be so sarcastic," she said in exactly Mom's tone. "How do you know it'll be stupid adult stuff? Something really . . . *cool* might happen!"

I was to remember her words later.

CHAPTER THREE

JUST BEFORE NINE SAL and I argued our way into the Grand Hall, both wearing cameras like real tourists. It was already crowded with people reading pamphlets. An elderly man wearing a tour guide button called us all to attention. He began to tell us about why this Grand Hallway was grand—who had designed it and stuff like that. He pointed out special details like the gold architrave and carved banisters.

I tried to pay attention, but most of it was incredibly boring. I started fooling around with my camera instead. Sally's eyes began to glaze over. We shuffled to the foot of the stairs and then slowly up them, staring at portraits or display cabinets as he pointed them out. We went up the stairs and into what he said was one of the longest rooms anywhere in the whole of the United Kingdom, the Long Gallery. It yawned out ahead of us.

It certainly was long—and very luxurious. Almost everything in it was crimson and gold. Fat gold cushions lay on red sofas. The walls were covered with crimson damask cloth instead of wallpaper. The many windows were shrouded over with red and gold velvet curtains, all held back with gleaming gold ties. It was like being inside a huge red mouth whose teeth are crammed with gold fillings.

All along the walls dozens of enormous portraits were lined up. I saw that the portrait nearest me was the most recent and walked up to it. It showed a crabby-looking man with mean, piggy eyes.

Lord Louis Minerva III

said a small brass plaque next to the portrait. He was no better in his portrait than in the flesh.

Next to him was a portrait of his sickly wife, who had died, the tour guide told us sorrowfully, within a few years of marrying him.

"I don't blame her," Sal muttered to me in a piercing whisper. "I'd want to die too if I was married to a sour old stick insect like him."

An elderly lady in the crowd overheard, turned around, and gave Sally a delighted smile. I left them saying their hellos and wandered down the line of paintings. Minerva lords and ladies, their eyes dark and haughty, stared down at me. Back into time they went, their clothes getting more old-fashioned.

There was a lady in a bustle having tea in the orchard. Next, a man fly-fishing from the lake jetty. Farther on, a woman in a frilly bonnet threw seeds to the white peacocks on a lawn.

Quite a few portraits showed indoor banquet scenes. The Minerva brigade were obvious gluttons—real pigs, in fact! Sal would fit right in with them. Each table was groaning with the food of the very rich. Snooty-looking Minervas sat and gazed upon all this plenty with small, piggy eyes.

I heard the rain start at the window and meandered over to it, yawning. There, on the wall next to the window, I found a portrait that made me wake up fast.

It showed a young girl aged about eleven, sewing in the garden. She wore a long red dress with huge bunched sleeves. Her white-blond hair hung in neat ringlets. I recognized her instantly. It was the girl from the maze last night.

LADY HARRIET MINERVA
IN THE ELIZABETHAN GARDEN, 1825

the brass plaque said.

So now my whisperer had a second name. Harriet Minerva. The crowd talked and moved all around me, but I stood rooted to the spot. It was as if the whole room, sights and sounds and all, had whooshed away from me. A cold, clammy feeling came over me as I stood looking at her.

This little girl had lived in 1825. Yet she had stepped out of the past last night and spoken to me. I remembered the thin, see-through face that had scared me so much last night. In the portrait her face was rosy cheeked, solid, and real. She had sat there sewing in the garden long ago, had tried to sit still as she had her portrait painted.

At last I turned away. I wanted to get out of there.

The nearest door, the one at the far end of the room, was blocked by a fat gold rope barrier. A sign that hung on it said: STRICTLY NO ENTRY.

On the wall of the corridor beyond, I could just make out an older tourist sign with an arrow: TO THE SCHOOLROOM AND OLD SERVANTS' QUARTERS.

I went back to exploring the room and slowly became aware of something else. All the artifacts dotted around the room, carefully placed to make it look as if it were still lived in by these long-ago people, were *adult* things.

There was a newspaper left on a table, with a pair of spectacles on top. There was a half-finished letter on the desk, its writing very small and adult. Complicated sheet music stood propped up on the small spinet, as if waiting for ghostly hands to come and play.

But none of these things related to children. There were no toys, no half-finished games of checkers, no picture books left lying around; no sign of children at all.

"Any questions?" asked the guide brightly, peering around at us all.

I put my hand up. The guide beamed at me in a sickly way. "Yes, young man?"

"Er, how come there are only adult things in here?" I said. "What about the children? Where are their things—toys and books and stuff?"

There was a pause while everyone checked to see if I was right.

"That's my brother," I heard Sal say to the old woman in her piercing whisper. "He's a bit stupid."

The guide cleared his throat and answered. "In the very best houses," he said, "children were expected to be seen but not heard. They would not have been allowed to play in this grand room at all, let alone leave toys around. They would spend most of their day in the nursery or schoolroom. And now we shall make our way to the Queen Anne chamber. If you all would follow me?"

He began to usher us firmly back toward the door. I glanced back to the sign that pointed toward the schoolroom. If there were any clues to the girl called Harriet Minerva, I figured they'd most likely be in there.

It was easy to edge to the back of the crowd as it made its way out. Sal was chatting to the old lady near the front, doing her I Am Cute act. I ducked under the gold rope barrier and darted out, into the forbidden corridor and along in the direction of the arrow. But there were no more signs to help me on my way.

I figured that if the schoolroom was near the servants' quarters, as the sign said, then I should just keep on going up. The poor servants always slept in the tiniest garrets and attics. So I set off.

At first everything was very clean. There was a faint smell of lavender polish in the air. But the higher I climbed, the shabbier the corridors grew. The windows were dingy, half shrouded by thick dusty drapes or by the dripping curtains of overgrown ivy outside. Through the chinks between the leaves, the intermittent sunlight reached in and lit up long fingers of whirling dust motes.

As I moved higher in the house, everything became more decrepit. I turned corners, climbing upward, until at last I opened a door onto a shabby landing and found myself on a familiar spiral stairwell.

I had come out in our own south turret stairway. One glance out the window showed me the now-familiar view, but from a little lower down. The stairs continued on, up to our rooms. So I must be . . . one floor below our rooms? I retraced

35

my steps back to the landing and opened another door.

Right at the end of this hallway was a tarnished brass plaque: THE SCHOOLROOM.

The door creaked as I pushed it open.

It was a large, dim room. On one wall were two blackboards, both blank. One of these was tall—the one for the teacher, presumably. The other was shorter and set lower into the wall, for a smaller person to stand and write there.

A child.

A dusty piece of white chalk lay in the groove under the smaller board. Nearby, a moldy rag hung on a rusty nail. I imagined a long-ago child, wiping this board clean of ABCs, and shivered. I hurried to the window to open the curtains and let some light in. The faded drapes shed years of dust as I drew them apart with a rattle and scrape. I started coughing. When I recovered, I saw a small row of battered school desks.

Now the room looked a bit more cheerful. But not much.

It was clear that no one had come up here for a very long time. The whole place looked completely forgotten. Here and there the wallpaper was peeling off and hung in great dusty furls, halfway to the floor. This revealed big faded sections of bare plaster.

My eye was caught by some ink marks left on a revealed section of old plaster. I moved closer and found a childish sketch of an ugly old woman. It had been sketched onto the wall a long time ago, even before the room had been wall-papered. It scared me.

She had straggly hair sticking out all around her head. Her back was bent. Her face was surrounded by seven candles, all lit. Dotted in and out of these candles were small frothy flowers. The woman's eyes were shut. Untidy letters were scrawled underneath:

FLOWERS FOR B.M.
MAY SHE REST IN PEACE.

Who was B.M.? I wondered as I stared at the drawing. I didn't much like that face with the closed eyes. Dead people had their eyes closed, after all.

I spotted a second penciled drawing a little farther down. This one was brilliantly done but weird. I knelt down to see it better. It showed a room with a high domed ceiling. The ceiling was painted all over with gods and goddesses, leaping around in a sky that held a crescent moon, a sun, and lots of tiny spiky stars. There was also a huge candlestick in the drawing of the room.

The sketch was labeled:

THE SKYTALE AND ITS SECRETS, BY ISAAC E.

I wondered what a *skytale* was and what "secrets" it held. I wondered how come the sun and the moon and the stars all shone at once in the same sky and where the domed ceiling might be.

From behind my back came the tiniest squeak. A mouse? I whirled around, nervous. Or even—God forbid!—rats? I *hate* rats; they make my flesh creep.

But the room yawned out before me, empty. It was probably just a mouse after all, I decided, behind the wainscot there.

I was just beginning to examine the drawings when I heard it again. A tiny squeak behind my back. But this time I recognized it and froze.

It was not the squeak of a mouse at all. It was a sound I'd heard before, the unmistakable sound of chalk squeaking against a blackboard.

I was unable to move. I couldn't turn around. I couldn't run. The blood felt as if it were draining out of my whole body as that sound went on and on.

Finally I heard it one last time, the grating sound of chalk, pressed onto the surface of a blackboard. Then there was a change in the light of the room, a sudden glare of sunlight. From the clock tower in the grounds, the clock struck ten. Suddenly I could move.

I whirled around and stared. The room was empty.

So too was the large blackboard, just as it had been. But the small blackboard was now almost filled with very neat copperplate writing.

It was a list of names and ages. After each one were three letters in parentheses: *Dcd*.

I knew what those letters meant. I'd seen them on the papers Dad had to sign after Mom was gone. I'd hated those three letters the *last* time I'd seen them. *Dcd*. For *Deceased*.

There were six names on the blackboard.

Harriet Minerva, 12 yrs. (Dcd.)
Oswald Minerva, 13 yrs. (Dcd.)
Nellie Minerva, 8 yrs. (Dcd.)
Edwina Minerva, 10 yrs. (Dcd.)
Thomas Minerva, 11 yrs. (Dcd.)
Beatrice Minerva, 12 yrs. (Dcd.)
Follow the Statues.

I ran then—ran fast—out of the schoolroom and back down the grand stairway to outside. And things happened quickly—much too quickly—after that.

I shouldered my way through the groups of tourists, and as I ran, I yelled over and over for Dad. I thought I heard his faint reply from the far south of the garden, beyond the lake. I remembered now—he'd said he'd be spending the day burning bindweed at the very edge of the estate. So I ran past the lake and through the Topiary Garden, heading in that direction. The tall hedge shapes flashed past me as I ran: a cockerel, a giant crown, a pyramid, the knight from a chess set.

As I ran, I kept thinking of that list of children's names, all deceased. I remembered the cold whisper of one of those children, Harriet, in my ear: *"I was born in eighteen hundred and fourteen."*

I ran on and yelled for Dad again. His reply came—a call, much nearer this time—from somewhere beyond those rhododendrons. I left the main path and swerved into them. Their scent rose up to meet me—the thick, heavy scent from thousands of fat crimson blooms. I crashed my way through them.

"Dad! Where *are* you, Dad?"

Then suddenly there were no more bushes. A small building stood before me. Gravestones, all slanting and lopsided, lined the pathway up ahead.

I'd found the forbidden chapel.

The outside chapel walls were overgrown with ivy. The roof was domed, with the base of a broken weather vane perched on top. The metal letters *N*, *S*, *E*, and *W* were still there, moving slightly in the breeze, but there was no weather vane figure above them.

As the wind nudged the letters back and forth, the rusted metal gave a brief tortured moan. It repeated over and over above my head. It set my teeth on edge.

Yet in the air there was the faint, comforting smell of woodsmoke, smoke from a garden bonfire. Relief flooded me. Dad must be here, working around the back maybe. The idea of him so close by made me less scared. Soon I could tell him all about it. I'd go right up to him. "Dad," I'd say, "something just happened. In the old schoolroom."

Then he'd stop work and come back to the schoolroom with me. He'd show me some faint words left there by the last person to use the blackboard long ago. He'd show me how in a certain light they could reappear dimly. Or something like that. He'd explain it all away. I grew calmer and went through the tiny gateway.

The gravestones stood in a small row, slanting this way and that. They were green and yellow with lichen and moss. I read the inscriptions, one after another.

LADY HARRIET MINERVA. 1826. BELOVED.

1856—LORD OSWALD MINERVA, OUR GENTLE SON.

LADY NELLIE MINERVA. FELL ASLEEP 1886.
GOOD NIGHT, GOD BLESS.

LADY EDWINA MINERVA. 1916. SORELY MISSED.

LORD THOMAS MINERVA. 1946. AT REST.

LADY BEATRICE MINERVA. DROWNED, 1976. RIP.

Right here, under my feet, lay all the children I'd just read about in the schoolroom. I felt the skin prickle along the back of my neck. One of them, the last, had drowned.

The thought of dead children lying under the earth made me shiver and move on. In an overgrown flower bed near the door were several tiny gravestones:

OUR LADDIE.

FAITHFUL JASPER.

BRINDLE.

WHITE MAURICE.

I read these names, and a lump came into my throat. The children had been laid to rest with their dead pets. But the last one made me think uneasily of that white cat I'd caught a glimpse of last night.

I walked up to the chapel door and listened. All was quiet. I opened the door and stepped inside.

There was a row of wooden pews all the way down the center of the building. I could see another door at the far end, left ajar. It clearly led toward the back garden of the chapel. I could still smell faint woodsmoke.

"Dad?" I called softly. "Is that you?"

I stepped farther in, and my mouth fell open. There, high up and festooned all over with cobwebs, was a domed ceiling I'd already seen, in the drawing in the schoolroom. The curves of the ceiling were painted all over with clouds and stars and a blazing sun and a horned moon. Running in and out through all this were the proud figures of many gods.

They leaped from star to star. They drove huge chariots or wrestled with one another in the clouds. They leaned back lazily on cushions and poured wine from golden goblets into their mouths. Each little group of them told another story. The story was sometimes of peace and sometimes of war. It was a tale painted in the sky.

The skytale, brilliantly sketched in ink by someone named Isaac E., whoever that was.

I wondered what secrets these proud figures could be hiding. I couldn't see anything obvious up there. The only other things in the building were a moth-eaten tapestry on one wall and a giant candlestick that stood near the front.

The candlestick was huge, far taller than I was. I instantly recognized it from the schoolroom sketch. It felt strange to be seeing these things someone named Isaac had seen long ago. Suddenly I needed to find Dad.

I walked toward the back door and pushed it wide open. Instead of seeing Dad standing there, all I found was a tangled back garden and, in the center, a statue of a girl with its inscription:

IN LOVING MEMORY OF HARRIET MINVERA
WHO TRAGICALLY DIED ON THIS SPOT
1826
RIP

There she stood with her long stone ringlets and those huge bunched sleeves. She was laughing, with both arms outstretched, happy.

"Follow the statues," it had said on the blackboard in the schoolroom. And now here was a statue of Harriet, the first name on that list of six names. How had she died here?

At the base of the statue I suddenly noticed a small square object. I took out my camera and photographed it in place.

It was a child's toy, that was all. Just a small square brick with the letter *B* written on its faces. Next to each *B* was a brown bear.

B for bear. But why had it been left here? And who had left it?

As I cradled it in one hand, the wind blew stronger and set the nearest tree branches swaying and thrashing. Leaves fell as if there were a sudden autumn. I dropped the toy block into my fleece pocket and looked up, puzzled.

All the trees farther away were still. Only the trees standing close to me thrashed in the wind.

After that I heard a weird sound, like many dry whispers.

It was as if thousands and thousands of pages were turning in some fusty old book of spells. Then slowly, as if in a bad dream, all the color began to bleed out of everything.

The sky lost its blues and turned a sickly off-white. The grass turned gray. The soft browns of the chapel's stone walls turned gray. In the end, everything—everything—was like some old sepia photograph, left over from the days before there was color film.

It sounds simple, the way I'm telling it, but it wasn't. There was something horrible about that wormlike color of grass and sky. There was something awful about standing in the middle of a strong wind that didn't seem to blow in my time at all. But then, a new fear came—like the one I'd felt that very first day in the garden.

Turn around slowly, I said to myself. *There is someone else here.*

I turned. My mouth went dry; my legs turned to jelly. The statue of Harriet had disappeared. In its place was a gray girl kneeling in the pale grass.

It was Harriet, a living, breathing Harriet. Her white hand reached out and picked strange, bleached bluebells.

My heart began to hammer in my chest. I wanted to turn away, didn't want to see this cold, pale girl with her white lips and silver fingers. But I couldn't move a muscle.

As she picked the nodding flowers, I heard a noise from far

above. It came from the roof of the chapel. Harriet heard it too. We both looked up.

On top of the chapel a huge weather vane was swinging in the breeze. Its metal cockerel swung this way and that, above the letters N, S, E, and W. The wind blew even stronger. From the weather vane came the shriek and creak of buckling metal.

As if viewing slow motion, I watched the weather vane begin to break in two. With a crack the central strut snapped. The cockerel hit the roof with a smash, slid clattering down the arched roof, and fell.

I knew it would fall on Harriet, not on me. She screamed, a bloodcurdling scream. I covered my eyes and heard a sickening thud as the weather vane hit her and knocked her to the ground.

I think I screamed then too. But I'm not sure. I wasn't sure of anything for a while. The next thing I knew, I heard a voice calling my name. It took me a moment to realize it was Dad.

He was shaking me by the shoulders as if trying to wake me up. "Jim! What is it? What is it?"

Then the grass was green again, the sky gray and blue. There was just the statue of Harriet before me, erected where she had died. And the small bear block in my pocket.

I clutched at Dad as he pulled me away, through the sweet scent of the rhododendrons.

CHAPTER FOUR

T HAT WAS THE AFTERNOON when everything changed, and it
had all to do with Dad's reaction. "You must have fallen
asleep and *dreamed* it all, Jim," he kept saying over and over
when we got back to my room. Dad made me lie down. He
covered me with a quilt. "Now, try to calm down."

I couldn't. I couldn't stop shivering. I hadn't dreamed it at
all, I kept trying to tell him; I hadn't even been *asleep*! But he
wouldn't listen.

My head hurt, and my thoughts kept whirling all around,
all crashing together. The memory of that sickening thud came
back to me. Her whisper, that night in the maze. The maze
made me think of Einstein. I grabbed at a sudden random
question I wanted to ask.

"Dad?" I asked through chattering teeth. "What day was I
born on?"

"What? Why would you ask that all of a sudden?"

"What *day* . . . was I *born*?"

"On a Wednesday."

"Are you sure?"

"Of course I'm sure. It was my day off. Now shh, you've just been having *nightmares*, that's all."

But people don't have nightmares when they are not asleep. Another question came. It was easier to think about Einstein than it was to think about Harriet.

"Dad, what does *autistic* mean?"

"Autistic? What's all this about? Have you heard something about Lord Minerva's son? Henry?"

I nodded.

"Well, autistic people can't quite . . . communicate like we can," he explained. "In fact they often can't look at us. They don't make eye contact. It's a condition."

I thought of the way Einstein never once looked at me during our meeting in the maze. It made sense.

"They're often very skilled, though," he continued. "Like, they can draw amazing things, or they are good with numbers. Sometimes they are geniuses. These autistic people are called savants."

Savants.

So. Einstein *did* seem to be Henry, with all his brilliant math and everything. Yet there were still so many questions running around my head. I closed my eyes and tried to think of anything other than Harriett's scream, and the sickening thud that was replaying itself like a tape over and over again in my head.

After a while Dad must have thought I'd fallen asleep. A few minutes later I heard him crying softly. He was whispering Mom's name. I lay there, eyes shut, appalled. And listening to him, I slowly made up my mind about two things.

First, I decided I wouldn't call him from his work again. No matter what happened. He'd said he'd been working at the edge of the garden when he heard my terrified yells, very distant. He was in the opposite direction, though, so it took him a long time to find me.

"But I smelled woodsmoke from your fire!" I'd said as he wiped my forehead with a cold cloth. "By the old chapel!"

"It must have just drifted across the estate," he replied. "The wind was blowing that way, after all. Shh now."

He was trying to sound fine, but I'd seen it in his eyes: a kind of horrible dread. He was terrified of something happening to me and Sal. After all, I suppose he would be. He used to think Mom would live forever.

As I lay there, eyes shut, listening to him grow quieter, I realized that his work was the only thing keeping him going. It was obvious, really. He was out at the crack of dawn and sometimes didn't come back until late. If he didn't need to eat and sleep, he'd probably be out there all night long, going grimly from task to task, pushing everything from his mind. He needed his work to hide in.

The second thing I decided may sound a bit funny, but it was true. In a way it wasn't just like Mom died. It was like Dad died with her too. It was as if I for the moment didn't really have any parent at all. Dad just didn't quite know what to do with us. Mom used to do all that stuff.

After all, this was his brave new start. My fears, my begging him to leave this place, were the very last thing he needed. If I wanted him to get back to normal, I'd just have to figure things out for myself. Any mention of seeing people from the past, and he'd go back to those few months after Mom went. He had longed to see her so much, he looked for her all over. Then, when she didn't come, he sat like a stone for days until the days turned into weeks. I'd do anything not to see him go back there. He wasn't the only one scared of losing the other two. As for Sal, I'd promised Mom to take care of her, to comfort her. So how could I tell Sal? She'd be too scared.

I couldn't tell anyone.

In the end Dad fell asleep with his head on his chest. His catnaps never lasted for very long. I crept into the kitchen and made him a strong cup of coffee with a lot of evaporated milk, just how he liked it.

He was just waking up again, yawning and scratching, when

I carried it in. He saw me standing there with the steaming cup and stopped, mid scratch. A helpless look came into his face.

"But Jim—I should be doing that for *you*!" he almost wailed.

"It's all right, Dad. Here—take it!"

After a second he took it and smiled weakly up at me. There we were, grinning at each other, but we both knew. He wasn't really "with me" at all. He was somewhere far away. With Mom.

Meanwhile, something horrible was happening here at Minerva Hall, and I had to figure it out myself.

Decision made. End of story.

So here I was.

Orphan Jim.

It was later that day, just after dinner. We were in our little curved living room, having just polished off Mrs. B.'s delicious lasagna. Dad had decided we'd eat all our meals, except for breakfast, up here. He said the kitchen was too hot after his long days outside, but we both knew what he really meant. He couldn't face talking to the other members of the staff. That made sense. Sometimes he hardly talked to us.

Anyway, I was just heading for the top of the spiral stairs, ready to go out again, when Dad called me back. Sal sat there, arms folded, looking mean and sulky.

"Don't just slink off again, Jim!" said Dad. "Spend some

time with your sister, all right? This is hard for her, too. And she could use a hand, sending these plates back down to the kitchen. Why should she do it on her own?"

He picked up a small leather box from a corner of the room and went off to his bedroom. I knew what that box held: Mom's photographs.

I even knew which ones he'd be looking at. First he'd stare at the wedding day photo—Dad with the weirdest haircut ever, Mom in a frothy white dress. Next, the one where Mom was dressing me in my new school blazer, the first day I went off to boarding school, her face all proud. Then the one of Sal, a fat baby on her knee, Sal dribbling a bit of spit off her chin. Mom is laughing and showing her a huge book. The book is filled with Egyptian squiggles.

That was her work. She was an Egyptologist.

Now I stared accusingly at Sal.

"You told Dad I won't play with you, didn't you?" I asked her.

"Well, you won't. You're always running off and you know I can't run as fast as you and Dad's always busy and it's weeks until we start our new school and I miss my friends and you won't play with me and I'm bored!"

Tears filled her eyes. A lump came unexpectedly into my throat.

"Oh, Sal, don't start again. I'll play with you after we've done these dishes, okay?"

"Promise?"

"Promise. Come on—you stack the plates and I'll work the pulley."

Sniffling, Sal slid apart the little double doors set into the paneling and piled all the dishes onto the dusty tray. Then she closed the doors, and I began to work the winch.

It should all be electric, of course; this hand winch system was from the days when there was no electricity, when dinosaurs roamed the grounds presumably. But the wiring had been declared too old and unsafe to use, and had been disconnected. Still, the manual winch worked fine. So I stood there cranking the handle as Sal watched. I imagined the tray of greasy plates being lowered into the dark, down all those floors. I thought of the spiders hiding in the shaft as my plates passed them by. Thousands of spiders, lurking there in secret.

Too soon there was a little jerk, and the crank jammed. I struggled to turn the handle, but it was stuck tight. The plates couldn't possibly have reached the kitchen already. As I worked to free the handle, Sal sighed. She wanted to go out to play.

"Is it stuck or something?" she asked.

"How should I know? I'll take a look." I slid open the doorway and leaned down.

"Oh, don't do that!" wailed Sally. "You might fall!"

"Don't be stupid, and don't start crying again. Just hold on to my belt!"

The light from our turret room didn't reach very far down. All I could see was the first few feet of the shaft gradually disappearing into darkness. The pulley chains by my head—quivering ones, old and dusty—led downward and upward. Above my head was the top of the shaft, its oily pulley wheels just visible.

I was just about to draw my head back in when I heard a sound from farther down the shaft. It was faint and deep, like the horrible sort of chuckle old people make in the back of their throats. An icy feeling clutched at me. Then the cackling stopped.

Had I imagined it? I must have! I forced myself to stick the whole top half of my body into the shaft and peer straight down.

"Oh, Jim, be careful!" yelled Sal. "What can you see?"

"Shut up for a minute!" My voice echoed back to me.

From far below a sudden bright yellow light revealed the shaft. I shielded my eyes, blinking. I could just make out the dumbwaiter tray, way down there.

It was ablaze with candles. This was so unexpected that it gave me a real shock. There were seven candles, all lit, standing around the dirty crockery.

Who would light candles in such a small wooden space? Who would risk starting a fire? Blinking, I got more used to the light, and my heart stood still.

There was a face looking up at me.

It was an ugly face, pale and wrinkled. It was the face of a very old woman. Long white hair, messy and wild, fell all over her head. Her mouth was grinning, and out of it came that horrible chortling sound.

But her eyes were completely shut. Even so, she seemed to know exactly where I was. She raised a gnarled hand and pointed up at me.

"The old one is watching you!" she said in a whispery, echoing voice.

The candles blew out, all at the same time. The shaft was dark and silent again. I pulled my head back in, slammed the small doors shut, and leaned against the wall weakly. I was finding it hard to breathe.

Sal stared at me, her eyes scared. "Jim? What *was* it? What did you see?"

I looked at her scared face and made an effort to pull myself together. I gave a shrug. "It was—it was nothing."

"No, it wasn't." She shook her head. "You're shaking. What did you see? *Tell* me!"

I pulled her away from the hatch and onto the stairs, making my voice sound as normal as I could.

"It was just Mrs. Benson. In the kitchen," I replied. "The mechanism must have jammed. She could have heard it stop and shone a flashlight up to work out how to free it. Her face just . . . took me by surprise a bit, that's all. Come on, what do you want to play? Catch?"

Sal nodded and followed me down the stairs. I forced myself to whistle, trying to seem fine. It seemed that Sal had accepted my explanation. I led her outside and played ball with her, but all the time my heart was hammering loudly in my chest.

It hadn't been Mrs. B.'s face at all. It was much, much older. Whoever it was, she scared me to death. And one of the other children who had lived and died before me had also seen her, I realized, and had sketched her on the schoolroom wall.

FLOWERS FOR B.M.
MAY SHE REST IN PEACE.

I recalled her cackling, her words. "The old one is watching you!"

She terrified me. Why were her eyes shut? Dead people have their eyes shut.

"Jim? Do you like it here?" asked Sal.

"Course I do!" I lied.

Sal began trailing me even closer that night. When we got back to the turret, she saw how red Dad's eyes were, from looking at his photos. A terrible lost look crept into her eyes.

She asked Dad if I could bunk down for the night on her

floor, and Dad said yes. She asked if we could keep the door ajar and a light on in the corridor, and Dad said yes. She asked if we could talk until she fell asleep, and Dad said yes.

He seemed exhausted himself and began snoring much earlier than usual. Sal and I lay there, heads together, both wrapped snugly in quilts on the floor. We listened awhile to the snores.

"Jim?"

"Mmm?"

"Do you *really* like it here?"

I stared at the wedge of light from the corridor and felt as if the whole world's troubles had settled themselves onto my back.

"Are you kidding? It's great! Better than boarding school, that's for sure! Why?"

She shook her head and began to suck on one of her braids. "I don't know. You just seem . . . scared?"

"Nooo! I've just have had a few nightmares lately. That's all."

"Nightmares? About what?"

"Oh, you know. The usual stupid stuff. I have to sing a solo in the school play, and I haven't learned the song. Or I get up onstage and find I'm standing there in my underpants. That sort of thing."

She gave a snort of laughter. "Which underpants? Your Christmas joke ones with the neon Rudolph on them?"

"Worse than that. Some horrible old gray pair with a big hole in them."

Another laugh. It had been a long, long time since I'd heard that cute little sound. I longed to hear it again.

So I told her every joke I could think of—all my best toilet jokes and then all the doctor-doctor ones I could remember.

"Doctor, Doctor, I keep thinking I'm a pair of curtains!"

"Well, pull yourself together!"

She laughed even though she'd heard them all a million times.

"Doctor, Doctor, I keep thinking I'm invisible!"

"Next?"

Then I tried all the knock-knock jokes I could think of.

"Knock knock."

"Who's there?"

"Water."

"Water who?"

"Water you doing waking me up at this time of night?"

They were terrible jokes, but she laughed until she had to stuff the pillow in her mouth. I pretended to do the same. When she finally fell asleep, her face peaceful in the soft light, I lay there awhile longer, listening.

A soft rain fell against the window. Somewhere nearby a gutter trickled and dripped. Deep in the body of the house the chimes of a small clock struck two. A few seconds later the mellow tone of the clock tower bell rang twice. Was the small clock too early? Or the clock tower bell too late?

Much later a fox cried out from somewhere near the lake, its eerie bark echoing. I thought back to the statue in the grave-yard. I imagined the stone Harriet as it would look now, sur-rounded by dark trees, arms outstretched to the moon, blind eyes pale and blank. I tried to think why a bear block might have been left at this statue but got nowhere.

It suddenly occurred to me that maybe Einstein would be able to tell me more about this whole creepy place. After all, he was the only person, since I arrived here, to have even men-tioned the children. "There are six children here," he'd said. And after all, he was a genius.

I settled down as soon as I'd made my decision. First thing tomorrow, straight after breakfast, I was determined to find Einstein.

CHAPTER FIVE

I LOOKED EVERYWHERE FOR Einstein all the following day. All I saw was rain and wet, miserable-looking tourists. But in the early evening, when the rain finally stopped, I spotted him at last. He was walking into the soggy Wildflower Garden, plodding through the cool evening air.

I stared after him from the kitchen door, watching that peculiar walk he had—as if his feet were always uncomfortable or something.

I slung my digital camera around my neck so that I'd look more like just one more late tourist and began to follow him through the gardens, toward the gatehouse. There were only a few stragglers left now; most of the visitors had gone home. I found him sitting on a bench near the entranceway. On his lap was a notebook in which he was busy scribbling. The squiggly lines looked like math problems. Even at a glance I could tell they were way beyond me.

"Hi, Einstein!" I said. "Or should I call you Lord Henry? What's that you're doing there?"

He kept his head down and wouldn't look at me.

I sighed. Great. Lord Minerva was a mean old man who spied on everyone and hated children. And the only other child here—of the nondead variety, that is—was a genius savant who hated eye contact. It wasn't a very good start.

I got the bear block out of my pocket and held it out.

"Einstein, stop ignoring me. Did you leave this at Harriet's statue, the one behind the chapel?"

His eyes flicked briefly to the block and away again.

"Bears and dogs, they are loud. This one, he does not like loud sounds. This one, he likes cats. Cats, they are not loud. Cats, they do what they want to do always."

It suddenly struck me that he would like cats; you can't get a cat to look at you either! You can't make a cat be friendly with you.

"Did you leave this block at Harriet's statue?" I repeated. He gave his head a quick shake and started on a new math calculation. I tried again.

"So . . . how come you're not at boarding school then?" I asked. "Mrs. B. thinks you've gone back to school."

He frowned. "This one, he did not go back to the school," he said tightly. "This one, he does not like that school."

Once again, when he said "this one," he pointed to his chest.

"You didn't go?" I said. "But . . . I don't get it. They certainly *think* you've gone!"

He began to write more numbers, his head bent low. A stupendous thought occurred to me.

"Wait a minute! Einstein, you're not—you're not skipping school, are you? Playing truant?"

"This one, he does not like that school," he replied at last. "This one, he hides and does not want to go."

I laughed. "You hate school? So you're playing truant? And now you're hiding from the adults? Oh, wow! Very cool."

I was genuinely impressed. There was clearly more to Einstein than met the eye. But he just went silent again.

"You'll have to go back in the end, though," I said. "Sooner or later. When they find out."

He shook his head from side to side and looked as if he might cry. "No, no, no!" he whispered.

It was clear he was desperate not to go back there.

"Okay, okay, calm down!" I said. "I won't tell them. I'll keep your secret. But now you have to do me a favor. So maybe you can help me with something?"

He considered this, then nodded as if we had a pact.

"I'm looking for some old records," I said. "Of children who lived here once. They all were Minervas. Nellie Minerva.

Oswald Minerva. Edwina and Thomas Minerva. Beatrice Minerva."

"A name, it has been missed," he said irritably. "The pattern of the list, it is all wrong. The first name in the pattern, it should be *Harriet* Minerva."

My heart leaped. Now we were getting somewhere! "You know the names!" I cried. "Have you seen Harriet too?"

"This one, he sees her. This one, he knows where her name, it is written down. All of the children's names, six names in total, they are written in the church."

"In the church? Do you mean the little chapel?"

He stood up then and stuffed his notebook into his pocket.

"The names, they are not in the little chapel," he replied. "The names, they are in the bigger church. The bigger chapel, it is this way."

He walked away as if he now had some purpose. I had to hurry to catch up.

"The small chapel, it has some letters in it too," he said. "But those letters, they are not the letters that belong in the children's names."

"No?"

He fell silent again. I frowned. I hadn't noticed *any* letters in the chapel. In fact, I hadn't seen any carvings or anything much in there.

"So what do the chapel letters say?" I asked.

"The chapel letters, they are flat letters, but they need to be curly letters. But the names of the children, they are this way." Einstein walked fast under the huge arches of the gatehouse.

"Henry," I said, "are we going outside the grounds?"

"Einstein!" he said sharply.

"What?"

"Einstein. This one, he likes the name Einstein. The name Einstein, it is like a German sum."

"How come?"

"*Ein*, it is the German word for 'one.' And the name Einstein, it has that word twice hidden inside it. *E*, *I*, and *N*. Two ones."

EIN . . . st . . . EIN. I considered this as we walked along and saw he was right. What a weird way of looking at things he had!

"Einstein, he was also a theoretical physicist." He nodded firmly, as if that clinched it. He stood waiting while I hesitated to follow him out.

Sal and I were forbidden to leave the grounds. We'd promised Dad. But I got a quick, fragmented feeling that if I didn't follow him now out of Minerva Estate, I might miss my chance.

"Okay, Einstein, let's go!" I said.

We walked along the road together. All the recent rain ran in little shallow gulleys at each side of the road, leaves and muck tumbling downhill. Einstein seemed as edgy as I was; I was scared of his changing his mind and going back. The only thing I could think of that might relax him was numbers. So that's how I ended up marching by his side reciting the only times table that comes easily to me, the tens, all the way to the village. "One ten is ten. Two tens are twenty, three tens are thirty . . ."

Instantly he joined in under his breath. We were almost up to two thousand tens when we reached the small gate that led to the church door.

A circle of white lilies was hung on the door, like a Christmas wreath bled of all color. It was festooned with black silk ribbon. From behind the door there came a somber hymn. We had walked slap-bang into the middle of a funeral.

The hymn ended, and the drone of the vicar's prayer came dimly to us.

Einstein led me up the side path toward a smaller side door. Quietly we sneaked in and found ourselves in a large room, hung all around with rows of vestments and a muddle of outdoor coats and jackets. We were obviously in the vestry.

Through an opposite internal door, the mumbling of the vicar and of the people at prayer was much louder. We'd have to be really quiet in here or we'd be heard.

Einstein hurried over to a glass-fronted cabinet. This held a row of enormous old books, each one attached to the inside of the cabinet by slender chains for security. The spines of the old books were labeled in fancy gold lettering :

BIRTHS

MARRIAGES

DEATHS

BAPTISMS

Einstein opened the cabinet door, reached for the third book, and laid it down. It was embossed in gold on the cover: *The Book of Deaths—1800 Onward.*

I began to turn the pages. Einstein, however, seemed much more concerned about the funeral service. He listened intently, his head to one side. He didn't seem to like the drone of the death prayers. There came the sound of pages being turned as the congregation found the next hymn. Several people cleared their throats. The doleful singing began again: a death hymn, a dirge. Einstein hurried to the outside door.

"Time to go, to go, to go!" he cried, wringing his hands in distress.

"Go? No chance!" I ran after him and hissed into his face, "We haven't found the names of the children yet! Show me where they are—hurry *up*!"

I dragged him back to the Book of Deaths.

"Come on, Einstein!" I said. "What years did the Minerva children die in?"

Einstein spoke in a soft voice. "The Minerva children, they did not just die."

"Did not die? What are you talking about?"

The droning voices began singing the next verse. Einstein reached for the Book of Deaths and flipped over all the pages at once, to show the inside back cover. He pointed down at some words, neatly penned there. I read through them, then grabbed my digital camera and photographed them.

They said :

Pray for the souls of the six Minerva children who died, one in each generation, at the hand of strange accidents. Their little bodies lie forever in that wretched land. Pray for those whose greed made these things happen.

Pray for that land where old things walk and whose water is impure.

In your mercy, reader, pray for Harriet Minerva. Oswald Minerva. Nellie Minerva. Edwina Minerva. Thomas Minerva. Beatrice Minerva.

May Almighty God have mercy upon them and upon us all. Amen.

Father Joseph Carey, Parish Priest, 1978

The organ started up again: a triumphant final march. Footsteps came toward us. They were coming in!

I shoved Einstein toward the door. The opposite door opened, and the priest entered. There was a pause, and then he yelled aloud, "What the *blazes*? Who on earth?" (We'd left the book out and the cabinet doors wide open.)

We didn't stay to hear more. We ran without stopping, all the way back to Minerva Hall.

As soon as we got back into the grounds, Einstein ran off without even saying good-bye. He just darted up a small path to the side of the gatehouse. I watched him go, wondering how much he really knew about all this and how I might be able to get it out of him.

I looked up at the sky and decided that it was still just light enough to go back to the forbidden chapel. I wanted to check out the "curly letters" Einstein had told me about.

It took me a while to find my way back there, but I managed it in the end. I shoved open the front door and went in.

It was all the same as yesterday, except that the small back door was now shut. I looked up at the skytale and still couldn't see anything apart from old gods and goddesses having a good time up there.

I went to the front of the chapel and stared at the huge candlestick. I examined it all along its length for letters but found none.

I finally examined the only other thing in the chapel, the tapestry. This was huge and shabby and very eaten away by mice and moths. The bottom hung in shreds, stained with damp. From what I could see, this tapestry wasn't anything much; it just showed a lot of huge, brooding trees by a lake. Their branches hung down almost to the water. But then I spotted something small in one corner, embroidered there like some sort of strange signature.

It was a shape made out of neat circles, six to make the circle and one in the center. As soon as I saw it, a strange feeling, a sudden stillness, crept into me. I felt this image was somehow important but couldn't think why. I photographed it.

The small dots could represent anything, I thought, anything placed in that shape. Marbles, or rings, or stones.

The name of the village suddenly leaped into my head: Sevenstone.

Might that be what this image represented? I counted the dots: seven of them.

Seven again.

Then I noticed that the whole tapestry was hung onto the wall by a narrow faded ribbon. At either end the ribbon was tied onto a wooden dowel that held the tapestry stiff at the top. Along the ribbon in one long line there were faded letters.

I'd found them!

Yet they were meaningless to me, oddly spaced with dashes in between. And these letters were certainly not curly.

EC-S-OEH----TE--SH-TIDRMTDEE-E-RBT
NEANIO-NMHRW-OM-OLRA-TEAOTIS-FOER---
ENK-C-A--TNIEETHEAG-TFO-DNO-NBFT-LNNE-
D-EETYO-O-T-UAEWA-E-SLTELKAEOCROE-RN-
NANAAHHY-GLM-GOEO-O-ETT-D-L---RH-
NTDR--NLOIE-FITNASEBNDEOTWHTI

They were gobbledy-gook. They just didn't make sense.

I gave up trying to work them out and headed back over the estate to the warm kitchen where Mrs. B. bustled about.

I liked it in here with her. The massive kitchen felt comforting and safe.

Mrs. B. briefly nodded my way as she set a muslin cloth filled with curd cheese into a colander over the sink. As she pressed down on it, thin whey came dripping out.

"Mrs. Benson, why is your village called Sevenstone?"

"My village?" she said. "Oh, it's named after an old stone monument that used to stand somewhere nearby. A stone circle. Pass me that weight from the weighing scales, will you? Not that one. I need the heaviest—that's it. And now—that plate."

I handed her the plate and watched her place it in the colander over the dripping cloth. She weighed it down with the five-pound iron weight. We watched the thin whey ooze out into the sink. Meanwhile, I thought of that image of seven dots arranged in a circle. Did it represent the name of the village? Or the monument the village was named after? I wondered. An old stone circle.

"I hope this will be a better batch than last time," Mrs. B. was saying. "Last time the whole batch was a tad too salty."

"What happened to it?" I said.

"I threw it away. A shocking waste of cheese!"

"Not the *cheese*," I said. "I meant, where was the stone circle?"

"Look, why don't you just read the blessed guidebook instead of pestering me with all these questions?"

She paused as she passed the dresser and reached for a thin book, nestled in among all the fat recipe books. She handed it to me.

Minerva, Sevenstone, and Thereabouts, it said.

"You can have that; it's an old one," she said. "They've changed the design several times now."

I opened the front page, and there, right under the title, was the same image I'd only just seen.

"Sevenstone!" I whispered to myself.

Mrs. Benson paused in the middle of measuring flour, her

lips pursed. "I wish you two would stop muttering to yourselves; it's just not *normal*! Your sister was exactly the same
earlier on!"

"Sal?"

"Well, yes—unless you have some other sister I don't know
about. She went slinking past the door, muttering and talking
to a dirty old toy block, of all things."

A dirty old toy block? The bear block? I'd left it in my blue
fleece pocket, hanging in the side kitchen. Sal must have taken
it, borrowed my fleece maybe; she was always doing that, too
lazy to go upstairs and fetch her own. Now she had the bear
block! I glanced to the window.

It was dark outside. The night seemed to press its face
against the window glass. I watched Mrs. B. begin to roll a lump
of pastry on the table. "Where did she go, Mrs. Benson? Did
you see?"

"I did not. I'm too busy to be keeping track of the likes of
you two."

"Well then, what did she say? You said she was muttering
something?"

"Talking to a toy block, of all things, saying she was going
to *take the bear home*, whatever that meant. She looked as
pleased as punch. I think you'd better go and find her, or she'll
miss supper. You can take my big flashlight if you want; it's
hanging behind the back door with the coats. Go on!"

72

She dismissed me with a nod of her head.

I tried the flashlight and was glad to see it was a strong one. Then I paused, thinking hard. *B* for bear. *Taking the bear home.*

I suddenly remembered about an old bear pit in the grounds. This, I figured, was where Sally might have taken the bear block—to "take it home." Where else would a bear belong?

I ran to the nearest tourist board with a map on it and studied it by flashlight. I tried not to notice the blackness of the hedges all around, and of the spooky statues everywhere. I tried not to think about the *old one*. Yet as I ran, I felt I could sense her somewhere out here with me, watching me through the dark.

CHAPTER SIX

THE BEAR PIT WAS JUST a huge circular pit lined with gray
stone. Nearby was a tourist information sign that read :

THIS NINETEENTH-CENTURY

BEAR PIT

WAS ONCE NEAR THE ANCIENT WILLOW BEDS,

NOW LONG GONE.

WARNING:

THIS SPOT IS STILL PRONE TO FLOODING AND

IS CLOSED TO THE PUBLIC IN TIMES OF HEAVY RAIN.

PLEASE DO NOT CLIMB ON THE BEAR STATUE.

I approached the whole thing by following a path on
ground level. It certainly was soggy! There was another path
going off to the side that clearly led higher up. This led to a

small stone tunnel, then into the pit itself.

The sandstone walls loomed around me. Looking up, I could just make out iron railings circling the top, where people used to stand and look down.

I stepped inside. I was scared already. "Sal? You here?"

A huge statue of a bear made me jump. It was rearing up on its hind legs with open mouth, as if it were growling. Sally sat at its foot, sobbing. I rushed toward her.

"Sal! Oh, Sal! What are you doing here, you idiot, sitting in the dark?"

She grabbed me. She was shaking all over. "I hate you!" she sobbed. "I really and truly hate you!"

"What have I done now?"

"You scared me, you know you did! I borrowed your fleece and found that lovely bear block thing. I came to put it at the foot of the bear statue, but it was lighter then, just going dark. And then I thought I heard you sneaking around in the bushes—those bushes, way up *there*."

She nodded toward the top of the high walls and the shrubbery that crowded there.

"You were sneaking around in the bushes there. I heard your footsteps! So I forced myself to go up and find you . . . because the bear pit was getting darker and darker and I was scared. But I called you and called you and you *wouldn't* answer, and then I got too scared, so I ran to hide—behind that!"

She flung out an arm to point to something directly above her head, where the dark railings circled the bear pit. I shone the flashlight up, and for a moment my heart stood still.

A small boy was standing at the railings, peering down at us. An instant later I saw that he was made of white marble.

Somehow I knew this would be the second child from the schoolroom list and from the Book of Deaths. Oswald Minerva. His stone eyes looked down at us. Cradled in his arms was a white marble cat. I kept my flashlight on him uneasily as Sal kept on talking.

"So I hid behind that statue, but you *wouldn't* come out to talk to me and I got more and more scared and I hate you and I'm going to tell Dad!"

I put my arms around her. Poor Sal. The thought of her getting involved in all this, hearing ghostly footsteps from another century, made me angry. Why did they have to bring Sal into it? She was shaking from head to foot. Or maybe it had been Einstein in the bushes? But it didn't seem likely.

"Come on, Sal, shh now," I said as calmly as I could. "Let's get out of here. Look, the top path won't be half as dark as this bottom one. Hold my hand. That's it—just follow me."

I led her along through the mud and up the slope toward the top railings, Sal sniffling loudly all the time. Together we walked up to the stone boy. Sal pointed.

"I crouched right behind there, hiding from you. But when

you wouldn't play, I ran back down to get the bear block, and it was gone! Where is it? Did you take it? I want it back!"

She began to cry again.

So someone had taken the building block by the time she got back to the bear statue. But who? And why?

"Sal, why did you stay in the bear pit so long? Out here in the dark by yourself?"

She grabbed the flashlight and shone it directly onto the statue. "Because I was too scared to walk past *him* again!" she gasped. "He looked real. He did, he looked real! It's just a cat he's holding, I can see it now with the light, but it was too dark before—I thought it was something awful and dead. And the darker it got, the more scared I got. And that lower path, the one you just came out of, was too dark, and after that I was just too scared to move *anywhere*."

Her chin began to wobble, and new tears formed. I suddenly remembered again the promise I'd made to Mom. "Take care of Sal," she had whispered from her hospital bed. And I had nodded, my heart hammering in my chest with love and sadness. I would do anything—anything—to take care of Sal. I tried to make my voice normal.

"It's only a statue, Sal. Look, it's just a marble statue of a harmless little boy."

Sal grabbed my hand and tugged me around to the back of the statue. "That's where I hid," she said. "Oh, *look*!"

77

She was looking down in surprise at something that had clearly not been there before. It was a circle of woven green leaves on thin boughs, glistening and wet. It looked a bit like a crown, made of . . . wicker? Woven into the front of it was a wicker figure, the size of a small doll.

I sensed it was very old. It looked like a plaything, something a small child might weave to pretend he or she was a prince or princess.

Yet it struck me that the strange central doll wasn't all that . . . cute. Not exactly. Its blank face was lean and had a hungry look about it. Locks of thin wicker hair sprouted out from its head. Its fingers tapered into thin little bony claws that were held outstretched in front of it, as if it were endlessly trying to clutch for something.

I looked down at it and felt uneasy. It struck me that it looked like something a witch might have once made, to use in some spell long ago. I didn't like this spindly crown with its strange wicker figure. Who had brought it here and left it for us to find?

"That wasn't there before!" Sal whispered. "Why are you playing all these *tricks* on me?"

I opened my mouth to reply, then stopped. I sighed. It was hard to know how to take care of someone, to really care for them.

Meanwhile, Sal was reaching down for the wicker crown.

"Wait," I said. "Let me take a photo first!"

I quickly took a photo. Sal shone the flashlight all around the base of the statue. "Look," she said. "Some words. Listen!"

She sounded much less scared now, and I realized that the more she found out about things, the less scared she got. It had been like that when Mom died. Sal had been outraged—truly, spectacularly outraged—that Dad and I had kept things from her. *"No more secrets—ever!"* she had screamed. *"I hate secrets. Hate, hate, hate them!"*

Now she cleared her throat and read the inscription aloud:

"LORD OSWALD MINERVA
WITH HIS BELOVED CAT
WHITE MAURICE.
1856
MAY HE REST IN PEACE."

Sal finished reading and put the wicker crown on her head. For some reason I didn't like this.

"Take it off," I said sharply.

She shook her head. "Why should I? I like it. And I don't have to do what you say. Anyway, where are you finding all these old things?" she asked. "Is this all part of some new game? I liked the bear block, and I like this wicker crown, but I hated it when you hid in the bushes and wouldn't come out. Don't do it again, okay?"

I stared down at her, not knowing what to say or what not to say, and turned away. Just then a feeling that I'd had before, a horrible feeling, began to overtake me. The back of my neck began to prickle. Color began to bleed out of everything. Everything began to turn gray and silver and white. *No, no!* I thought. *Not here, not now with Sal!* But the colors continued fading until even the yellow flashlight beam was a ghastly white. Fear spread through me. I knew that Sal and I were no longer alone.

I closed my eyes tightly. The last time everything had gone all monochrome like this, I'd seen the way Harriet had died. Dread filled me. I didn't want to see Oswald die. I opened my eyes and stared in shock at where the statue had been not a moment before.

In its place was the gray, see-through figure of a boy. It was Oswald. At his heels, weaving in and out, was a cat. White Maurice. It wasn't raining where they were. I glanced at Sal, but she didn't look as if she could see him. She was playing with the crown.

Oswald was stripping a small stick of its bark and sharpening its end to make a spear. He was humming as he worked. Maurice purred and nudged at his legs.

The ghostly tune came to me, and my heart turned over. I knew this tune well. Mom used to sing it to Sal when she was very small. "Greensleeves."

Oswald's spear was finished, clean and sharp. He began to

walk slowly around the outside of the empty bear pit, dragging the spear along the railings one by one to make it clang in time with his song. Ahead of him was a gap where the railings had broken. But Oswald didn't see it. He stepped nearer, singing the words now:

> "Alas, my love, you do me wrong
> To cast me off discourteously,
> For I have loved you so long,
> Delighting in your company!"

He was now five feet away from the gap in the railings. Dread filled me. I reached out my hand toward him. "Stop," I whispered. "Please stop!"

Sal stopped fiddling with the crown and stared up at me, her mouth agape. Meanwhile, Oswald got closer to the gap. Purring all the time, Maurice followed him.

> "Greensleeves was all my joy.
> Greensleeves was my delight.
> Greensleeves was my heart of gold
> And who but my Lady Gr—?"

His song was cut short. He lost his balance. His eyes opened wide, and then, with a small, kittenlike cry, he fell into the bear pit below, still carrying the spear.

I knew what would happen, what must have happened to him long ago. He had fallen onto the spear he had just made.

I felt a tugging at my sleeve and turned to find Sal's blue eyes wide. "Jim!" she whispered. "Who were you talking to? What did you see?"

I tried to speak but couldn't.

"Jim! What was it?" She sounded on the edge of hysteria.

I took a deep breath. "Nothing. Well, something. Just . . . a rat. I thought I saw a rat down there. You know how I hate rats."

"Stop *lying* to me!" she yelled.

My heart was racing. The statue was back in place now, the colors returned to normal, but I felt something new. I felt as if we were being watched by someone else. Someone even more frightening than Oswald had been. It was an awful feeling.

"We have to go," I said. "Quickly! Follow me!"

I dragged her away from the bear pit and, holding her hand, ran back toward the house. To reach it, we had to pass the lake. Its surface was cold and dark. We ran on.

"Slow down, Jim! Let go—you're hurting me!"

Then, out of nowhere, the geese and ducks gave a cry of alarm in the water beside us. I heard them scatter, flapping and panicking, over the lake. I peered into the darkness, shining the flashlight that way.

The old woman stood there on the water, her face toward us. I slid to a halt. My legs almost collapsed.

"Stop it," cried Sal. "Stop standing there all white. You're scaring me! Oh, please let's just get back to the house."

She tugged me farther toward the lake. The hag stood there, hunched and bent, but Sal didn't seem to see her.

She was lit with a ghostly silver, as if she were a mirror that reflected the moon. But there was no moon visible in the sky. I thought of the small crown we'd just found and its tiny figure that looked as if some old witch had made it. Was she a witch? She began walking toward us.

I screamed. Sal screamed because I had.

I turned and dragged Sal back along the path, running almost all the way to the bear pit. Then we took another path that I figured must lead the long way around to the back of the Hall and to the kitchen garden.

It seemed to take us an age to reach the house, an age of dark shadows flitting, of Sal and me gasping as we ran. Then we were at the back of the Hall, and a small door, lit by one emergency light, loomed up before us. We ran through it and made our way to our turret stairway. Back in our living room we stood with our hands on our knees, panting.

I felt sick. Sal turned my way, her face utterly petrified.

When she finally spoke, it was in a small, tight little voice. It was exactly the same sort of voice, I realized suddenly, that

Mrs. Benson had used, days earlier, when she said, "You heard a cat? In the locked room?"

"Jim? That wasn't you I heard moving in the holly, was it?"

"No, Sal. It wasn't."

"Who did I hear then?" she said in a voice that rose with hysteria. "Who *was* it? And what did you see *after that*?"

She ripped the strange wicker crown from her head and flung it onto the floor. She burst into fresh tears. "I hate this place!"

I picked up the crown with its strange headpiece and shivered. "Come on, Sal," I said. "Let's go to my room. Wipe your eyes now. I have things to tell you."

She gulped and swiped the tears from her eyes. Then she nodded gravely and tucked her hand into mine.

The feel of her small fingers slipping trustingly into mine felt like a great weight landing on my shoulders.

We sat together on the floor in my room, wrapped in our quilts, for the second time in two days. I hid the wicker crown on the windowsill, behind the curtains. I didn't want Sal to freak out every time she saw it.

Dad still wasn't back; he'd gone off to the town to fetch gravel and supplies. I felt strangely relieved by this. I didn't want him to see Sal so white and scared. I didn't want his questions, on top of hers.

84

I told Sally parts of it all. I had to. She was way too clever to trick. She listened solemnly, her eyes as wide as saucers.

"So you see, Sal, *someone* left these old things by the statues," I said. "The bear block and the crown thingamajig. But it wasn't me."

"Is it the other child? The one I heard moving in the bushes?"

"Probably," I said, although I didn't really know. Somehow I felt it hadn't been Einstein. It must have been one of the dead children, I decided, playing tricks on Sal. Maybe they were like typical young children, as full of mischief in death as they must have been in life? Perhaps they played tricks like this because they enjoyed it, like setting the garden swing swaying and creeping around in bushes just to scare us. I hated seeing Sal getting involved.

"But *why* are they leaving things for you to find?" she asked.

"Well, what if—what if there's some sort of secret here, Sal? And someone wants it to be . . . sort of *uncovered*? So they're leaving clues and stuff?"

"Like . . . some sort of treasure trail?" she asked.

"Yes, exactly like that!"

"Okay, then, but why such funny little things? Why a bear block? Why a willow crown?"

"Willow? I thought it was wicker."

She rolled her eyes as if I were hopelessly stupid. "Willow *is* a sort of wicker! It's the old name for what baskets and things were made of."

"Oh."

"It's funny that the things left are both *toys*," she said to herself. "A building block and a crown. I wonder why."

Perhaps it's because they're the ghosts of children, I thought again. *Perhaps toys are all they can leave?* But I couldn't use the word *ghost* at all; Sally would freak out if I did.

I shrugged. "Well, I'm sure they're friendly, whoever they are."

"Really?"

I nodded. "Yes. We've just got to join everything together, to find out what's going on. Didn't you say last week you wanted to be a famous detective? And you won the Scrabble tournament at school three times in a row! So you should be good at all this."

"Yes, but this is different," she replied, looking upset. "This is scary and *weird*!"

I didn't dare tell her about the hag with the closed eyes. I didn't tell her about Einstein, either. She'd only tell someone and get him into trouble. Sal can do puzzles, but she is famously hopeless at secrets.

She quietly began to cry. "I want Mom," she whispered. "I want Mom!"

I put my arm around her and swallowed hard. "I know, Sal. So do I."

After a while Mrs. Benson's voice came calling from the top of the stairs. "James? Sally? Are you two up here?"

"In here, Mrs. Benson!" I yelled, relieved. Mrs. B. had a way of cheering things up.

Sally gestured helplessly at her swollen, red eyes and dived to lie down under her quilt, face to the wall. Just as Mrs. B. clattered her way in, Sal gave a series of light and totally convincing snores.

"There you are, Jim!" said Mrs. Benson. "I've been worried about you. Your dad phoned. He's stuck in the next valley. All that rain made the ford rise too high; he can't get the car through. He'll have to wait a few hours till the water goes down again, so he asked me to look in on you. Why didn't you come and tell me you were safely back? Is your sister all right?"

She nodded toward the snoring hump that was Sally, and her expression softened a little. "Where did you find her?" she asked.

"In the bear pit."

"That old place? Children always seem to love that bear pit—I can't think why! I think it's cruel myself, the way they used to keep them tethered up like that. Anyway, here, I brought you these. One each."

From her big apron pocket she brought out a packet,

wrapped in greaseproof paper. Peeling the paper away, she held out two large Cornish pasties. They were still warm.

"Oh, thanks!"

She placed them on the end of the bed, walked over to the window, and looked out. She stood there quietly with her back to me. From Sally came a soft little snore.

"Mrs. Benson?" I asked. "How long have you worked here?"

"Too long," she said. "Why?"

I racked my brains for the name of the most recent child from the Book of Deaths list. "Well, do you remember a little girl from 1976? That was in your time, surely? I think her name was Beatrice. Beatrice Minerva."

A long silence followed this. It went on and on. I decided she couldn't have heard me. Then she spoke again.

"It's not good to live in the past too much," she said. "People always seem so unable to let the past go, always asking about the old ways."

She fell quiet again. The way she'd said "the old ways" made me think that she knew far more about them than she ever wanted to.

"What old ways?" I asked.

Another shrug. "Just things that used to happen here, long ago. Things to do with the pagan ways and the summer solstice. The solstice has always been a strange time for us one way or another. It's nearly the solstice now."

88

"The solstice?"

"The longest day of the year. The summer solstice. It's in four days. That guidebook I gave you mentions it. People come and stay in all the hotels and pubs around about now. One way or another there's always someone asking about the past."

She sounded upset. But I had to know, so I pressed on. "And Beatrice? Did you know her?"

She nodded. "Beatrice was Lord Minerva's niece. It was all so . . . sad. There's been a lot of sorrow here. Sometimes I think the sadness will never go away!"

She gave a big sigh, then turned back to me with a big, bright smile. "Anyway, you just enjoy those pasties, all right?"

I nodded. "We will. Thanks, Mrs. B."

Oops, the "Mrs. B." had slipped out at last.

She put her head to one side. "Mrs. B. My hubby used to call me that," she said. "I haven't heard it in years and years! It's nice to hear it again. Oh, well, good night then, Jim. And good night, Sally, I hope you manage to get to sleep soon."

There was a pause; then a little voice came from under the quilt. "G'night, Mrs. B."

She left us alone with our pasties.

I waited until Sal was snoring—real snores this time—then went over to the window. The grounds looked peaceful. The calm face of the lake reflected the chilly blue pinpricks of stars.

From some unseen corner of the garden of statues a peacock gave its sudden, harsh cry. It was a peaceful scene, very calm.

But far over the distant hills, heavy gray clouds stealthily began to cover the stars. Storm clouds, dark and dangerous, were gathering.

CHAPTER SEVEN

SAL AND I SAT ON A bench in the Rose Garden, one on either side of Dad's lunch box and flask. Nearby, Dad and two undergardeners were shoveling gravel from huge plastic sacks and raking it onto the damp paths.

By my side Sal was studying the guidebook Mrs. B. had given me, the willow crown by her side.

"What exactly are you looking for, Sal?"

"Dunno. Anything about the bear pit. Or about willow. The notice at the bear pit said that it was built on the site of the edge of the old willow beds. So willow might be important, because of the crown thing. Hey, take a look at this picture! Oh, yuck. What a hag!"

She folded the back page of the booklet toward me and a tiny shock ran through me as I recognized the face drawn there. It was wrinkled, and its eyes were shut. White hair stuck wildly out. I tried to sound normal.

"What does it say about her?"

"'Found carved on the culvert stone on Sevenstone village green from where the spring used to emerge,'" Sal read aloud. "Carved on a culvert? It can't mean that. It's cruel! Isn't a culvert a baby hare?"

"That's a *leveret*, you nut!" I said. "A culvert is a place where water comes out, I think. Is there anything in there about the name of the village itself?"

She flicked through the booklet and found a page. "Only a little. Are you sitting comfortably?"

We briefly exchanged glances. This was what Mom used to say before she read us anything out loud.

"Then I'll begin," said Sally. "'Sevenstone is a charming example of a medieval village, with many clues to its ancient past within its boundaries for the keen historian to find. The village itself was named after an ancient stone circle, now, sadly, lost to time.' End of quote."

"Is that all?" I said. "But I already knew that anyway! Mrs. B. told me all that. Who wrote this stupid booklet anyway?"

Sal flipped to the front and read aloud: "'Compiled by Miss W. E. Everard, Culvert Cottage, Sevenstone.'"

"Miss W. E. Everard. I wonder if she's still there in the village."

"Doubt it," she said. "This guidebook was written twenty-five years ago, it says here. She might even be dead by now."

Thinking of the village made me remember the church. Around my neck hung the camera—I hardly ever went anywhere without it—with its photo of the Book of Deaths inscription. I thought of those six names. I'd already seen the way two of them had died. Harriet and Oswald. Would I have to witness the deaths of the other four? A sort of pattern seemed to be emerging here, as if each child who had died here long ago were trying to nudge me toward something. Something about the old ways maybe. Something that might help me . . . to do what? To do what that first whisper had told me to do? Find the Seventh?

As for the old one, the hag, even the thought of her made my stomach turn over.

"Okay then," Sal said, "let's think." She sat back and knotted her long braids together. She says it helps her to concentrate. "The first statue you found was by the forbidden chapel, yes?"

"Yes. Harriet's statue. And that had a bear block by its base—"

"—which led to the bear pit, which was built—"

"—at the start of the old willow beds. And there was the second statue—"

"Oswald's," she said.

"—Oswald's . . . and *that* one had the strange willow crown at its base." I finished off.

"And you said that the tapestry in the chapel has a small circle of seven stones in one corner. And Sevenstone is the name of the village. So maybe someone is trying to tell you something either about the village or about the stone circle. In the meantime, it seems that willow is also important."

"And candles."

"Why candles?"

I'd forgotten—Sal hadn't seen the candles in the dumb-waiter shaft.

"No reason," I said. "I just got mixed up."

She gave me a funny look, and I turned away to watch Dad hurl spadefuls of gravel about. He looked tired out already. He suddenly called for Sal, and she ran his way. The undergardeners, I noticed, seemed to be clocking off work already and heading back to the Hall. I heard Dad ask Sal to run to the potting shed and fetch a wider rake. Sal ran off, muttering, "Wait for me!" as she ran past.

Unexpectedly, Einstein appeared from behind the Rose Garden wall. He just stood there by the bench, looking, as usual, down at his shoes. Alarmed, I glanced over to Dad, then pushed Einstein behind a privet. "Are you crazy? Get out of sight. My dad'll see you! Einstein, look at this crown thing. Look at it! Did you leave it at the bear pit? Do you know what it is?"

I held the willow circlet out to him, but he just turned his face into the privet and began to examine the leaves closely. I tugged him around to face me again.

"Einstein, look at it. Did you leave it at the bear pit?"

"This one, he does not like bears. This one, he likes cats."

"But were you there last night, at the bear pit? Hiding in the bushes?"

He shook his head. "This one, he does not go to the bear pit. But this one, he has seen these crowns before."

"You have? Where?"

"The crowns, they are written about in books. The crowns, they represent an old spirit. One, two, three, four . . ." He was counting privet leaves, no longer interested. He was so exasperating!

"Okay then—stay there while I go ask my dad something. I'll be back in a minute, okay? Just *stay out of sight*!"

I wandered over to Dad, trying to look casual. "Dad?"

"What now?"

"Do plants and trees have a sort of . . . special significance? Different jobs and stuff?"

He straightened up and nodded. "Of course they do. You know that! Herbs and the like. Some heal; others are poisonous. Why do you ask?"

"What about willow? Does that have any special meaning?"

Dad tore open another bag of gravel and began raking it out.

"Willow. Let's see now. Willow grows near streams, on

riverbeds, by any moving water. It used to be used to make brooms and brushes and wicker and other things. Which reminds me, I must clean out the potting sheds; there are hundreds of baskets rotting in there."

"Baskets?"

"Willow baskets. They're a fire risk now, as dry as tinder. I'll maybe have a bonfire tomorrow. Where on earth is your sister with that rake? These undergardeners are driving me crazy; my back's killing me already." He continued grumbling. "They might be young and strong, but they're all part-time workers. I can't get all this done on my own."

"Dad, do you know where the willow beds used to extend to, exactly? The start of them was where the bear pit is now. But where did they end?"

"I'm not sure," he said. "I just know that there's something about willow that makes the locals think this valley is unlucky."

"Like what?"

"Oh, I don't know!" he snapped. "For Pete's sake, how long does it take one girl to fetch a rake? Go get her and make her hurry up. Fetch a couple. You might as well both give me a hand here. Go on, quick!"

As I ran away, Einstein was still there behind the bush, counting the leaves with a rapt expression on his face. He'd left by the time we got back with the rakes.

So we had to spend the rest of that day running and fetching and helping Dad as he spread the gravel. It was hot work, and all day long I was troubled by a strange sort of . . . *waiting* feeling. Everything felt tense, badly balanced, as if at any minute something would fall out of place and bring something terrible with it. The feeling wouldn't go away. If anything, it grew.

Later I sat on my bed toweling my hair dry after my shower. Sal walked into my room without knocking, went to the mirror, and began undoing one messy braid.

"Still trying to figure out what that crown thingummy means?" she asked.

I nodded.

"Well, cheer up," she continued smugly. "Because while you have sat there getting nowhere, I myself have been rather brilliant!"

"Oh, yeah? That'll be the day. How come?"

She undid the other braid, grabbed my comb—my comb!—and began to comb her hair as she chattered on.

"Well, I got to thinking. If there is some mystery here, to do with seven stones, then the village of Sevenstone is the most obvious place to go. I mean, it's the biggest link we've had so far, to tell us about any of this. So hurry up and get ready."

"Get ready?"

She began to braid her hair neatly. "That's what I said. Come on—we're going to the village."

"But Dad said we're not allowed outside the grounds!"

"I know, stupid. That's why I've persuaded him to come with us. A nice evening walk."

My mouth fell open. "Dad? Dad is actually going to tear himself away from his work, to take us to the village? How on earth do you get him to *do* such things? He'd just say no if I asked him!"

She snapped the elastic bands back onto her hair and shook her braids into place. "He did say no. You give up too easily. I just looked sad and waited. It worked. He said it'd be good to have a walk while we still could; there are bad storms forecast apparently. You have to have *charm*. You have none. I have lots."

She dug the comb into my hair, left it stuck there, and flounced out.

Sal skipped most of the way to the village, hanging on to Dad's hand, excitedly chattering. *Stop talking at him!* I thought. *He'll get annoyed. He'll want to turn around and go back!*

But she rattled on and on, asking all about the hedgerow flowers. What was this called, this pretty white one? What sort of tree was that? How can you tell them apart? Questions, questions. She was so annoying.

Still, it felt amazingly good to walk away from Minerva

Hall, to get away from that place with Dad walking between us. The farther away I got, the lighter I felt. I just wanted to keep on going when we got to the village, to walk right through it and out the other side, never to go back to that creepy old Hall with all its restless dead people.

There was the unmistakable smell of fish and chips in the air as we walked past the church and into the village center.

"Mmm, smell that!" said Dad. "Shall we have some chips?" We followed our noses all the way there.

It was a tiny fish-and-chip shop, right on the edge of the village green. Several bored-looking teenagers hung about by the benches near it, kicking at cans and laughing too loudly. We bought our chips and moved far away from them, to sit on a low stone wall and eat while they were hot.

The greasy food made my stomach churn. I gave Sal my share and wandered a little way off, following the line of the low wall. I wanted to get away from Sal's chatter.

A bit farther up the lane, I glanced back and saw Dad nodding to an old man, out walking an even more decrepit-looking dog. The man stopped to chat, clearly enchanted by Sally, who could wrap old people around her little finger. She put on her cute face and smiled up at him sweetly. The man, I noticed, seemed to be wearing something long, with a tie waist. Was it a *dressing gown*?

Then Dad moved around in front of him, and I walked on.

After a minute or two I passed a tiny pub, its sign swinging slightly in the breeze. THE WILLOW AND LANTERN, said the sign.

The picture on the sign was of an old-fashioned lantern, surrounded by a small crown of willow. The crown had a tiny witch figure. My heart gave a great lurch. I wished I could go in and ask about it.

As I walked past the pub, still following the line of the wall, I heard the tiniest trickle of water somewhere close. I realized that the tiny water sounds were coming from the other side of the stone wall.

I knew that the village culvert was the place where water had once emerged and that it had some ancient carvings on it. And I could hear just a trickle of water—so it stood to reason that this might lead to the culvert itself.

I peered over the wall and saw only a mass of pale cream flowers and tough yellow grasses. I climbed up the wall and jumped down the other side, straight into an unexpected boggy mess. Cold, smelly water splashed me right up to my knees.

I swore loudly. I had somehow jumped into the lowest, boggiest place in Sevenstone! The mud and water sucked at my sneakers and the lower half of my jeans. I looked wildly around for a way out of this bog.

Straight ahead of me, a thin path led up a slope and into some shrubbery. A small graceful tree stood there, its leaves hanging down. I realized it was the same sort of tree as the ones on the chapel tapestry. Was it a willow?

I heard a voice, as if the tree had answered me. Then came a scrabbling. Someone was forcing a way through tangles. The willow boughs parted and a thin face appeared. It was a middle-aged woman, with short spiky bright red hair, all gray in the front.

"I thought I heard a splash!" she said cheerfully as she held out the hooked end of a walking stick toward me. "I was worried it might be my father who had fallen in—it wouldn't be the first time. Here, grab hold of this, and I'll pull you out."

She clung to the walking stick as she pulled me up the bank. I was drenched through. Black, stinking mud coated my jeans up to my calves.

"Oh, dear!" laughed the woman. "What a scowl! And what a mess you're in! You'd better follow me."

She began to tug me along a tangled back garden and around the side of a small cottage, chattering all the time.

"Have you seen an old man and a dog? Did they pass you? He may—or may not—be wearing his dressing gown. The man, I mean, not the dog. Your shoes are squelching a bit, aren't they? It's all that rain the other night. It builds up somewhere under the village and floods us out at times. We'd better get you inside and get your feet dried—you're shivering. I won't take no for an answer. So who do you belong to? Or are you here all alone?"

We had arrived at a gate in front of the cottage. She shaded her eyes against the setting sun and peered back along the boundary wall.

"There he is! And just as I thought, in his dressing gown! Is that your family, talking to my father? Is that your little sister?"

I suddenly noticed that the woman held a huge chisel in her other hand. The tool glinted sharply in the last rays of the sunlight. As she yelled for her father, I wondered if she was okay. It struck me that she looked very odd, with that short, spiky red hair, streaked all over with a soft dove gray. Her earrings were huge blue parrots. One of them hung upside down, seemingly nibbling her ear.

I could just see the headlines. CHISEL KILLER STRIKES AGAIN! MAD PARROT WOMAN ESCAPES FROM LOCAL PRISON!

Dad and Sal and the old man came up. A small terrier came running up the garden path, barking wildly. The old man's dog on the other side of the wall joined in loudly. The noise was awful.

Dad looked shocked to see me standing squelching in the garden on the wrong side of the wall. The woman pointed down at my shoes.

"I'm afraid your son has found the true drawback of this village," she yelled above the dog noise. "Shocking drainage and stagnant water! The culvert hasn't flowed properly for years. His shoes will smell awful soon. Why doesn't he take them off and rinse them under my garden tap? His trouser legs are a bit of a mess too. I'll dig out something for him to wear while they dry. I see you've already met my father, Jacob. Come in, come in. Just ignore the dogs; they'll get bored soon."

She ushered us and the dogs to the back door, where she pointed helpfully to a garden tap. I turned it on and stuck my muddy feet under it. The cold water set my teeth on edge.

Meanwhile, they all trooped in through a tiny back door. When the water got too cold to bear, I squelched my way toward them and peered in.

It was immediately obvious why the woman had been carrying a huge chisel. She was a sculptor. Pieces of carved marble stood here and there: cherubs and moon faces and a giant toad. Her kitchen was full of stone dust, and two doors stood open, leading away from it. Through one, all I could see was a tattered old dog bed, the plastic kind, chewed up all along its rim. Everything was covered in a thin film of gray stone dust.

On almost every wall, it seemed, small bunches of herbs and flowers hung upside down, drying. Even these were covered in dust. I realized that the grayness at the front of the woman's hair was from stone dust, not from age. She threw her walking stick and chisel down, put the kettle on a stove, and began to make tea.

Meanwhile I noticed the small sign nailed to the cottage door: CULVERT COTTAGE.

Sal saw me register this and smiled at me excitedly. I knew what she was thinking. *Culvert Cottage was the home of the woman who had written the small guidebook Mrs. B. had given me!*

"Are you called Miss W. E. Everard?" asked Sally suddenly, jumping straight in with both feet.

"Not anymore, no!" She looked astonished. "But that was my maiden name. How on earth did you know?"

"The guidebook you wrote." Sally grinned. "The old one. We have a copy. My brother's doing a project, for history. All about the Hall."

I was? First I knew about it!

"My daughter," said the old man suddenly, "is a meadow."

Puzzled, we stared at him.

"A widow, he means," said his daughter. "My husband died eight years ago. So I am a *widow*!" She shouted this last word very clearly at her father.

"That's what I said!" he replied indignantly.

Dad had a tense expression on his face. Sal spotted this and stepped in before he could look for reasons to leave.

"Jim's history project," she said again. "He has tons of questions he wants to ask about it. Don't you, Jim?" She gave me a meaningful stare.

"Oh, um . . . yes! Tons," I answered lamely.

"Well then, you'd better take your shoes off and come in

and join us. Grab that towel. Here, you can step into the pantry there and put these on. They're all I've got. Sorry about the color, but they're clean!"

She threw me a pair of dusky pink tracksuit trousers. Sal giggled. I gave her a baleful glare and went into the small pantry to change.

"What does the W. E. stand for?" I heard Sal ask.

"What?"

"Miss W. E. Everard? Your name on the guidebook?"

"Oh! Willow Evelyn." She groaned. "I know, I know, it's a stupid name. Everyone just calls me Eve. But the name Willow has been in the family forever, and I got stuck with it. I felt more sorry for one of my cousins; he got called Lanthorn!"

"Lanthorn!" Sally laughed in full I Am Charming mode. "If my parents had called me Lanthorn, I'd have run away."

"Oh, me too," Eve said. "*Lanthorn* is an old-fashioned word; it just means 'lantern.' Before they had glass for lamps, they used horn, *lantern-horn*. Here, chuck me your wet jeans, Jim. Now come sit near the fire. Those tracksuit bottoms don't look too bad on you after all."

Sal exploded into more giggles. I glared at her again and sat down.

Eve Everard was clearly one of those women who can make tea, clear up several chairs, get people seated, feed the dogs, and set shoes and clothes to dry all at once. I handed her my dripping jeans, which she rapidly squeezed out and then threw into a rickety-looking dryer. She grabbed my shoes from the doorstep and quickly ripped up several sheets of newspaper from a huge plastic tub labeled "RECYCLING." She stuffed the newspaper inside my shoes, put them to dry near the coal fire, and passed me some cookies.

So that's how we first got talking: Miss Willow Evelyn Everard That Was, her father (Jacob), and us. We sat together around the messiest kitchen table I have ever seen—filled with lumps of clay and plaster and wire models of this and that—and conversations began flying about. Both Eve and Jacob, it seemed, had to have at least three topics of conversation at once, or they got bored. Dad looked annoyed and stood quietly, clearly embarrassed to be here.

Eve chattered on pleasantly. "So what do you want to know, Jim, for your project? Father, don't put your elbows just there—you're squashing my clay. Mr. Brown, please sit down—there in the rocking chair, just throw the cat off. Sally, pass Jim the cake, will you? Get *down*, Fido!"

At this last yell, both dogs leaped guiltily from their separate armchairs and slunk under the table.

"She named both of them Fido," Jacob told Dad, rolling his eyes as if his daughter was just too much in general. "Said it'd be easier for me to remember. I remember it all right! I remember all sorts of things!"

"Fido?" Dad smiled, looking from one to the other of them. He didn't quite seem to know what to make of these two strange people. It was as if he'd just walked into a birdcage filled with exotic birds that now kept batting against his head.

"I mean," said Jacob to Dad, "it's not very . . . original, is it? FIDO?"

Dad colored up and stammered something about good old-fashioned dogs' names. Eve laughed easily, shoving a stray lock of hair out of her eyes. Her fingers, I noticed, left a gray streak of stone dust down her temple.

"Actually, it *is* quite original," she said. "It's spelled P-H-I-G-H-D-O-U-G-H. Check their collars if you don't believe me. Now, Father, sit down and take one of your pills; you're getting overexcited. So, Jim, what was it you asked me for your project?"

I hadn't. I hadn't had the chance. But Sal spoke up.

"Your cottage is called Culvert Cottage, isn't it?" she said. "So is the culvert—the old culvert, that used to be on the village green—is it in your garden or something? I couldn't see it anywhere in the village."

Eve rummaged in the table drawer for some pills and passed one to her father. Then she handed him a Rubik's Cube.

"Fiddle with that till your medicine starts working," she said to him. "It'll calm you down, it always does. Sugar, Mr. Brown? What were you saying, Sally? The village culvert? Oh, yes. It's in the front parlor. Go in and take a look if you like."

Sal and I stared at each other, bewildered, but Eve just gestured toward the second small doorway and laughed.

"It is—honestly! Go in and see it. It used to be on the village green at the bottom of my garden. That's the part you jumped into, Jim. It wasn't always smelly and boggy. It used to be lovely, to judge from the old drawings of it, with a wide stream and fish and everything. But then it all changed; it dried up to a trickle, but water has a way of finding its way downhill. The village got terrible drainage problems, with water emerging any old where—especially in my cellar! They had to dig up the road and culvert stone. My mother said she wanted the stone, and the whole village agreed. She was a bit of a character, my mother."

Her father poured his tea into his saucer and slurped at it, spectacularly loudly.

"Excuse our manners," said Eve. "We're such slobs! Anyway, my mother had the workmen build the whole culvert stone into our fireplace. 'It's a good thing the fire dried it out,' she'd say, 'or we'd all be walking on water!' My father has lots of strange gifts, but walking on water isn't one of them. Now then, Mr. Brown, how are you settling into the Hall? Is Alicia being good to you?"

"Alicia?" said Dad.

"Alicia Benson. She lives just along the lane from us. Her bark's far worse than her bite, you know. She was telling me that Alfred—he's the son of Mr. Benjamin, the owner of the pub here—was wondering if there were any full-time gardening jobs going at the Hall. He's a good person. Maybe you could interview him?"

They began to talk about Alfred who wanted to be a gardener. Soon they had forgotten us. So we crept through the tiny doorway and peered into the parlor.

Sure enough, the mantel of the fireplace was made from a huge oblong of stone. On it were the carvings we had already seen in the guidebook. But the guidebook, we saw now, had shown only half the carving.

There were two parts to it. We stepped past the chewed-up plastic mess that was the dogs' bed and took a closer look at it all. First there was the top section with the hag's blind face surrounded by small leaves. There was a small vase of creamy flowers placed on top of it.

The second section had been laid into the floor as a hearthstone. It was carved with words. Sal got there first (I was a bit tangled up in a Phighdough), and she read it aloud:

> "Betwixt the worlds
> Of life and death,
> Bring meadowsweet
> With its baby's breath.
> Bring candles bright

And rounds of willow.
Bring light again
To my stone pillow."

"Good thing I took your camera," she whispered, pulling it out of her fleece pocket. "Take a picture, quick, before she comes in!"

I did, complaining all the time that I wished she'd stop using my stuff, but I almost wasn't quick enough. Just as I put my camera away again, in breezed Eve, tugging Dad along by his sleeve.

"I'm *so* sorry about my father," she was whispering to Dad. "He can seem quite rude."

"No, no!" protested Dad, clearly embarrassed. "It's fine, fine!"

"How is it fine for him to spit in your tea? Of course it isn't! But his pills will start working soon. I didn't notice he'd slipped out straight after his bath—I was busy getting the cats off the dogs. He always gets restless when he's missed some of his medication."

Dad shrugged helplessly. He noticed us there and came over, relieved to be able to stare at the strange fireplace too and pretend he was terribly interested in it.

"Did he *really* spit into your tea, Dad?" asked Sally in delighted tones.

"Be quiet," said Dad. "So, what have you two found?" He

stood reading the words of the verse aloud, making a big show of them to get over his awkwardness. Dad never was very good around women, I realized.

"How interesting! What does the verse mean?" he asked the still-flitting-about Eve. Now she was trying to stuff a fluffy heap of knitting into a knitting bag. Several balls of emerald green wool rolled under the sofa. Dad rescued them and tucked them back into the bag.

"Oh, thanks," she said. "I'd hate to lose these balls of wool. I've been knitting this sweater for so long, they don't even *make* that shade anymore. Just shove the whole bag up on that shelf, will you? The cats will disembowel it again if not."

Dad obeyed, then turned back to us. He regarded us quietly, his eyes moving between my face and Sal's.

"It's time to go home," he said meaningfully. "It's quite a walk back. Aren't you tired?"

We both shook our heads no. He looked crestfallen, as if we'd really let him down.

"Eve?" asked Sal hurriedly. "Will you tell us about the culvert stone? Whose face is that? Is it an old woman or an old man? Why are the eyes shut? And what does the verse mean?"

Eve came and stood before the fireplace. She read it all over again, quietly.

"Yes," she said, "it's good to stop and read it again. When it's here in your parlor, you tend not to see it after a while."

I stared at the small blue vase of flowers perched at the center of the mantelshelf.

Not see it? Yet someone had left a vase of flowers here, and recently. The flowers were fresh. You could even smell them in the room. They were a frothy creamy yellow, with minute flower heads set in tall spears. They were the same sort as the ones that surrounded the boggy ground, I realized. Sal reached out and touched one flower head with the tip of her finger.

"This is pretty," she said. "What is it called?"

"It's meadowsweet," said Dad.

"Just like it says in the verse?" asked Sal.

This brought a little nod from Eve. "Your dad's right. It's meadowsweet. It used to grow all over these valleys, especially at Minerva. Just smell it! The scent of it will get stronger and stronger, all through the night. Sometimes you wake up and feel almost drunk with it. As to the verse, it's very old, many centuries old even."

"Where does meadowsweet grow now?" asked Sal.

Eve gave Sally a shrewd sideways look. "Are you interested in wildflowers and herbs?"

Sal nodded.

"I expect you get that from your father." Eve smiled. "Meadowsweet grows near water, near springs and marshy bits, like at the bottom of our garden. As I said, Minerva used to be filled with meadowsweet. Willow, too, when there was running

112

water there. Both are important healing plants. There are some interesting carvings about it all, in the hothouses on the estate. That's where the willow beds ended. I've spent hours in that main hothouse, studying the plants and—"

There came a crash from the kitchen. We all hurried back out. Jacob sat there, his head on his chest, asleep. Both dogs stood on the table, gulping eagerly and guiltily at the cookies. The plate was on the floor, broken into three.

Dad took this as a sign we really must go, even though Eve quickly cleared up and offered us more tea and some more cake. But Dad insisted, speaking in jerky little sentences. *We've overstayed our welcome. Thank you for drying Jim's jeans. No, they're not quite dry. But he'll wear them just as they are. I hope Jacob is much better soon.*

I changed back into the hideously damp jeans and even wetter shoes. The jeans were still warm from the dryer. Steam began to rise from me. I felt stupid, but it was better than the pink tracksuit.

Eve ushered us toward the door. She looked spent, as if all of Sal's questions and her own bustling about had emptied her somehow. "I'll say good night now," she said firmly. "Come again!"

The tiny back door banged shut, its little sign, CULVERT COTTAGE swinging.

When we got back to Minerva Hall, there was a note from

Mrs. Benson perched on the bottom step of the turret stairs. It was stuck into a toast rack so we couldn't miss it.

> *The Master would like to see you and the children, in his office, as soon as you get back from the village. Please pick up the kitchen telephone and dial 143. His butler, Montague, will answer it and direct you there. Please turn all lights off in the kitchen after, except for the small blue lamp. Thank you.*
>
> *Good luck,*
>
> *Alicia Benson (Mrs.)*

CHAPTER EIGHT

O NCE AGAIN LORD MINERVA sat before us, wrapped up in
a huge dressing gown, his brandy glass in his hand. Once
again he gave us a warm mock welcome.

"Mr. Brown—and your children! Come in, come in! I trust
you had a pleasant trip to the village?"

Dad looked surprised.

"Oh, you can't keep anything secret with *that* damned
woman around. Alicia Benson?" said the master. "She's well
known for it! I wouldn't tell her much—not if I were you."

He gestured toward a sofa that stood at a slant by the fire.
Dad sat. We began to join him, one on either side, but his nibs
spoke again.

"Not you two. You two can stand . . . over there, near the
desk."

We obeyed. To judge by Sal's face, she was as scared as

I was. His nibs went on.

"Right, Brown. I'll come straight to the point. I'm afraid your children have been rather making a nuisance of themselves."

Dad looked our way. "They have? I'm sorry to hear it. Perhaps you would care to explain?"

"It would be my pleasure. They have been wandering about Minerva and its grounds as if it were an amusement park set up entirely for them. I will not have children wandering unaccompanied all over the place. Do I make myself clear? I also have reason to believe your son has been down to the village. Something there was meddled with, and as for here, something has already disappeared from Minerva."

"Such as?" asked Dad. "Although if you are suggesting either of those things has anything to do with Jim, I'd have to object. My son is no thief, sir."

"No?" Lord Minerva's eyes were mocking, sarcastic.

"No. And both my children are forbidden to leave the grounds. Neither of them has been to the village until I just took them there myself. Have you been there on your own, Jim?"

I racked my brains. Einstein had been there with me, so I hadn't exactly been there alone. I shook my head.

Lord Minerva fiddled with the buttons of his wheelchair control and whirred closer to me. He stared into my face. "Do

116

you go sneaking about other people's property? Have you been down to the village?"

"No. And I am not a thief!" I blurted out.

"Well, I admit, I'm concerned. After all, what if you go wandering about in my coin rooms? The bone china rooms? Each collection here is priceless, and you do seem to have a nasty habit of roaming around, snooping. So you've never been down to the village before?"

There was a smug look on his face that I didn't like. He reminded me of a spider weaving a web to catch a fly in.

I shook my head. "No. Honestly I haven't, Dad!"

A horrible look of triumph crossed Lord Minerva's face. "Oh, really? Then I suggest you take a look at this."

He reached toward a small side table, then held out an old-fashioned videotape, the kind still used in some older security systems. It was neatly labeled in red ink with what looked like a date. Dad stared at it, puzzled.

"Take it!" said Lord Minerva. "Put it into the first console on the desk. Press play. Then stand back and see for yourself, Brown."

Slowly Dad reached out to take the video. He brought it over to the desk and slotted it into the first machine there. He pressed play. A grainy image flashed onto the screen, flickered and danced all over the place, then steadied. We all stared at it, mesmerized.

At first it showed some place I didn't recognize. A lane,

117

with trees and an ivy-clad wall and the very tops of what looked like tombstones poking above it. Then the scene changed to show a huge, heavy doorway under an archway.

I saw where it was, and my heart sank. It was the church. But it couldn't have security cameras watching it, could it? The very thought turned my stomach. I already felt sick from the thick cigar smoke in the room.

On the small screen the heavy church door suddenly opened, and a miniature me ran out. I ran fast, along the little pathway through the graveyard and out into the lane. Straight after that, the vicar came chasing after, garments billowing everywhere. He opened his mouth and called some soundless, angry words. Dad stood watching it all as though thunderstruck.

With a small whirring sound, Lord Minerva touched the control panel on his wheelchair and glided over to the desk. He stopped the tape and turned to Dad with a sickly smile.

"The church is kept under close security guard. It has valuable gold plate in it, belonging to Minerva, of course. I very generously let them use it for special occasions. So you see, we can't be too careful. The priest phoned me and said someone had been fooling around in the vestry. Well, Brown, what do you have to say for yourself now?"

Dad opened and shut his mouth, helplessly thrown.

Lord Minerva nodded and continued, smiling all the time.

"As I have just shown, your son is a liar, and so he could just as well be a thief. I should like you to ground him. From now on, I expect you to keep him with you at all times, as you work. As for your other child, your delightful daughter, I should like you to put her into the care of my head cook. The woman might be a gossip, but she can at least make herself useful and keep your daughter out of harm's way. Do you like cooking, girl?"

He shot this question at Sally. She shook her head, looking terrified.

"Nonsense! All girls like cooking in the end. There are all the chutneys and jams and the like to prepare for the gift shop, and Mrs. Benson could do with your help. Lord knows, Brown, your children need *something* to do until they start school. I shall even pay them a small sum for learning their trade, for I myself would not expect to work without pay. That way you could get your *own* job done and your children could learn skills and earn a little pocket money also. That seems to be a most agreeable solution all around, don't you think?"

Dad stared at him like a fish out of water. He turned to look at me with a lost, helpless look. I knew then that he would agree to what Lord Minerva was saying. Tonight he had for once left his work and tried his best with us. And as soon as we got back from that trip, I'd been caught lying to him. This fact had hurt him more than anything else.

Lord Minerva whirred back to the fireplace and pulled the

silken bellpull there. His butler came in at once, as if he had been hovering right outside the door.

He probably had, I thought bitterly. Watching. Listening, eavesdropping, snooping around! Then I remembered that I too had been caught snooping. Lord Minerva was right.

Suddenly I hated him, really hated him, for showing Dad I had lied. I hated his butler with his impassive face. I hated the secrecy and the eyes of the closed circuit TV cameras all over this spooky place.

"That's all nicely settled then." Lord Minerva smiled. "Montague, show them out. Then bring me some red wine from the cellars. I fancy a little nightcap before bed. That 1947 vintage my father laid down should do very nicely. I rather feel like celebrating."

Dad pushed us to the door, his face like thunder.

Back along the hallways we went, Dad's face set like stone. Once back in our turret, he told us to get ready for bed and to *hurry up* about it! He stomped off into his bedroom.

What a night it had been for him: first Eve and her batty father and then his nibs! I bumped into Sally coming out of the tiny bathroom.

"You *idiot*!" she said through gritted teeth. "Now I'm in trouble too, and I didn't sneak into any churches! What on earth were you doing at the church? Is that the day I couldn't find you?"

120

"Oh, what does it matter? I'm grounded, that's all that matters!"

"How can *you* be grounded? You'll be outside! It's me that'll be grounded, stuck indoors, cooking jams!"

I opened my mouth to reply, but Dad yanked open his door and glared at us. We scuttled to our rooms.

I woke up far too late for breakfast, aching all over. I felt shivery, and my throat hurt. I told Dad I felt awful and had a cold after being drenched the night before, but he was tight-lipped and insistent. I was to stop complaining and come help him with the bonfire. Sally was already hard at work in the kitchens, he said. He threw me an apple and a banana—"Breakfast!" he barked—and led me outside to the potting sheds.

It is awful to work for so many hours with someone who is angry with you. I hated it. Dad made me sort flowerpots into different sizes and clean the cobwebs off them. I had to be careful with them: no breakages. They were very old clay and terra-cotta, he said.

They were filled with spiders, too. It seemed as if every spider in Minerva had hidden there. So the morning passed with spiders in pots and anger in a hundred glares Dad sent me. I kept my head down. Every so often, when Dad was turned away, I glanced over toward the hothouses and could have screamed with frustration. There were so many questions I needed to answer! Like why did the dead children want me to find the Seventh? The Seventh what? I thought of the locked door and wondered if that had anything to do with it all. If it did, I didn't know how to get into it. So that was a dead end.

As for the toys the children were leaving for me to find, they seemed to be sort of clues. It was as if they were setting me a strange treasure hunt. But instead of treasure at the end, would I find something terrible and scary? The hag, maybe? I hated not knowing all this. And with Dad by my side, now I wouldn't be able to sneak off back down to the village, to see if I could unearth something about that intriguing pub name, the Willow and Lantern. He kept me hard at work.

But after a couple of hours he seemed to relax a bit. He stood regarding my shelves of neatly cleaned and sorted flower-pots.

"You've done a good enough job with them," he said grudgingly. "Now follow me. I want to burn those baskets before the rains come again."

As he led me to the main potting shed, I saw that the sky still had that gathering, gloomy look. There were huge banks of clouds, building up above the garden of statues, brooding over our heads as we went about our work. It was as if everything were collecting its strength up there and might come crashing down on us at any minute.

Dad opened the creaky door of the long potting shed. The

smell of musty tomatoes and mold reached me. Everywhere there were vast tottering towers of rotting baskets. We carried them out, trailing cobwebs.

As we piled up all the rejects into a huge bonfire, I suddenly realized that these were the same baskets Dad had mentioned the day before. They all were made out of willow, just like the willow circlet. There were hundreds of them. A thought struck me.

"Dad? Why so *many* baskets?"

Dad stamped several broken baskets flat with his heel and threw them on the pile. "Basket weaving used to be quite an industry here, I believe. Many of the willow workers had to leave the area after the willow beds went."

"What made them go?" I asked.

"Not sure. Something about the water changing, I think. Pass me those newspapers, will you?"

I handed Dad a pile of old papers and watched him crumple them up. He stuffed them into the nooks and crannies of the basket mountain, lit a match, and set the paper alight. It took fast, and soon the old wicker began to crackle loudly. The smoke rose, thick and dark.

All the time we tended the fire, I worried about Einstein. Something was bothering me about him. I concentrated hard on what it could be. Suddenly obvious, it leaped out at me.

There were six dead children, all sons or daughters of Minerva

Hall. *And the only child of Minerva left here now was Einstein.*

Was he next? Was he the Seventh child? If the other six had died from freak accidents, then was he due to meet with one too? Mrs. B. had seemed uneasy about the old ways and the solstice. What had she said the old ways were about? "Things to do with the pagan ways and the summer solstice. The solstice has always been a strange time for us one way or another. It's nearly the solstice now."

Was Einstein maybe in danger of something happening on the solstice, due in two days? I hardly knew him, had met him only a few times. Yet he seemed so lost, so submerged in his own little world, so unable to defend himself. How could I help him?

Dad took only one short break when he sent me to the side door to bring two cups of tea Mrs. B. had said she'd make. Sal handed them out to me, looking all flustered from the hot kitchen. She had a huge smudge of flour on her forehead.

"Your face is all black and smudgy!" she said.

"So? Yours is all white and smudgy! And did you find anything out from Mrs. B.?"

"Not a chance. We're too busy making the perfect hot-water pastry—for ten zillion pork pies."

"Is it fun?"

"Are you kidding? *Deadly* boring. Lord Snooty Male Chauvinist Minerva is quite wrong: All girls do *not* learn to like cooking in the end! I'd much rather be with you and Dad, making a bonfire. I kept myself from dying of boredom by making little people out of raw pastry. But I kept eating them all. I feel awful now—like I've eaten a pillow or something."

She rubbed her stomach ruefully, then stepped outside for a moment to cool down.

"I've been thinking," she said.

"Oh, really? I hope it wasn't painful."

"Shut up and listen. It's about those willow beds. Eve said that willow grew best near *running water*, didn't she?"

"Yes, Sherlock. So?"

"Well, if there used to be huge willow beds here, then there must have been a lot of running water here too at one time. Yes or no?"

"Yes. And your point is?"

"Well, if you find out where the water *used* to run on the estate, like streams and rivers and stuff, and why they disappeared, then you might find out some more about the willow and why it's important."

Mrs. B. called for her, so I carried the tea back to Dad. It must have been the quickest tea break in the history of the world.

The weather turned rainy again. I worked quietly, thoughts whirling. Dad worked beside me, lost once again in himself. The grief in his eyes touched my heart. He had a lost look, like Einstein did.

125

It occurred to me that I didn't even know exactly where the truanting Einstein was hiding out. I'd never seen him in the Hall. A few days ago I'd overheard Mrs. B. tell one of the maids that Lord Henry's room in the west tower could use a good cleaning now that he was back at school.

I stopped work a moment and gazed toward the west tower. I'd never once seen him walk that way. He always seemed to be heading the *other* way, farther to the south of the estate. When Dad went back to the greenhouse for something, I grabbed the site map out of his backpack and checked it.

To the far south there seemed to be nothing but woodlands and a few minor paths that led to a large copse. Behind this copse was a row of small buildings, marked, OLD STABLE BLOCK—TO BE DEMOLISHED.

I shoved the map into the backpack as Dad came back. Would I ever get away from him? How could I possibly find out anything when I was stuck with him all the time?

"I wish this storm would hurry up and just get it over with!" Dad grumbled as he grabbed a wheelbarrow. "I'm hot and sweaty; then I'm cold and sweaty. And this stupid soft drizzle, it wears you out!"

I knew what he meant. The fine rain would not stop. It seemed to drain us. It dappled the lake surface and left tiny silver penny shapes in it that grew outward. Then the wind came gusting along and mixed them all up again.

If only I could get down to the pub in Sevenstone and start finding some answers to all my questions! But it seemed impossible. Then finally, just before lunch, something happened that seemed to offer a solution. Like most things that can solve a knotty problem, this began deceptively simply. Dad stood up and put both hands to his back, wincing.

"I'm just too old for this," he said. "All this heavy work. Really, I should be planning new beds or doing the hothouse work or just supervising all this stuff. It's all right having all these undergardeners, but they're just part-timers. By the time they get here every morning, a lot of the heavy work is done."

With a sudden flash, I knew exactly what to say—something that would help both Dad and me at the same time.

"What about getting someone more permanent, someone *local*?" I said as I raked the gravel flat. "Didn't that woman, Eve, didn't she say that the son of the pub owner wanted a gardening job here?"

Dad massaged his sore back and frowned. "So she did! What was his name again?"

"Alfred. Alfred Benjamin."

"That's the one."

"Mrs. Benson told me he was really strong," I lied. "As strong as an ox, she said. He works behind the bar but hates it, she said; he always wants to be outside, not stuck behind a bar. He's there at the pub today, she said."

127

"She did? He's there today?"

She hadn't said anything remotely like that, but the lies just kept coming.

"Yes, and she said she's too busy to teach Sal in the kitchen for the whole day, she'd only be in the way. She's got the big meat order for the weekend to go through. So Sal can't be with Mrs. B. all day anyway. But never mind—I could watch Sal. Why don't you go to the pub and interview him?"

"I don't know. I can't leave you two here, not after all that from his nibs last night."

I got really crafty then. I knew I had to pretend to want to stay here alone. "Oh, Dad, we won't get into any trouble. Honest, we won't! We could just . . . explore or something."

"You could not! You'll both just have to come with me. And you'd better behave yourselves! I know they serve food, so presumably they must be open for lunch. All right, go get your sister. We'll have lunch there and see if I can get some permanent help for all this heavy work."

In the car as we drove to the Willow and Lantern, my small excitement grew. The willow crown that had been left at the bear pit was identical to the one I'd seen on the pub sign. I sensed I was at last about to learn something important, something that would help me find my way through this mystery.

CHAPTER NINE

THE PUB WAS ALMOST empty. It had a crummy old pool table and a pockmarked dartboard with no darts.

We ate first. Sal and I had scampi and fries. Dad had baked trout in fennel. Then Dad asked about Alfred, and he turned out to be the weedy man who had served us the food. He came from behind the bar and sat with Dad while they talked about boring garden things.

Alfred seemed delighted about all this. He kept shaking Dad's hand and grinning. He was thin and didn't look all that strong. Dad gave me a quick puzzled look. But I dragged Sal off to look at the old pictures on the walls.

There were the usual landscapes and hunting scenes. Some horse brasses. Nothing interesting. The owner sat staring at a newspaper at one end of the bar. "Don't touch anything now!" he said to us, peering sternly over his glasses.

Sally nudged me and nodded toward the wooden wall panels that lined one side of the room. They were carved with willow circlets, and a witch doll figure. Beside this there was someone I knew all too well: the old woman, her eyes closed, her face deeply wrinkled. Finally there was an old-fashioned lantern with a candle inside and rays shooting out. Above all this there was a shining sun and a sickle moon.

I thought of the skytale in the ruined chapel. That too had both the sun and moon on it in the same sky.

"Well, what are you waiting for?" whispered Sal. "Ask the owner about it!"

"No, you ask him. You can turn on the charm. I can't."

"I'm not surprised, with a face like that. *Try* to look a bit less moody!"

With that, she sidled up to him. When he looked up, she gave him a radiant smile and began to work on him. I watched him melt right in front of my eyes.

"Is that carving about the pub name?" she asked. "Why is it called the Willow and Lantern? Did you name it that?"

He climbed down from his barstool and came to stand by our side. "It's been called that as far back as I can remember. And that's a very long time. I was born in this house—back there, in the kitchen. My mother went in to get a bowl of porridge and came out with me in her arms instead!"

"I bet she was really pleased." Sal smiled. "You're better than porridge."

The man sat down by the fire and smiled from my face to Sal's. I tried to look pleasant as I pointed toward the wall panels. "Why are the sun and the moon out at once on the carving?" I asked. "Isn't that unusual?"

"That? Oh, that just depicts the summer solstice, the longest day of the year. It's soon, you know. The sun and the moon were especially worshipped on the summer solstice. I do good business then. People like to sit outside till late."

"Why the willow circle thing?" asked Sal. "Is it a crown?"

"That's a very good question, young lady, and it has a very interesting answer. So if you sit down, I'll tell you all about it."

We sat opposite him, and he pointed up to the carving. "That willow circle thing, as you call it, is indeed a crown. A solstice crown. They used to be made from willow, by the local lads and lassies, to be worn for the solstice rites." He sat back and gave Sal a wink. "And I know you're going to ask what the solstice rites were, so let me save you the breath. I've done a bit of research into it all myself, you know—I like to find out about things—and I found out that in this valley every solstice there used to be a ritual that happened at an old stone circle. It's all about a willow spirit that the druids believed in and kept happy. That's who the little figures on the crowns are meant to be, the willow spirit. Some say the figures also represent water

131

spirits. Either way, it's not male or female, but something like a mix of both. The legends say it was in charge of the rain and sun and whether the harvests were good and all that. People had to do whatever the land spirits wanted."

"I don't like the sound of that," said Sal.

"Good thing you aren't a druid, then! Anyway, the solstice crowns were a way of honoring this spirit, to keep it happy."

"Why?" I said quickly. "What would happen if it wasn't happy?"

"Who knows? There's not a lot written about it. Maybe it'd kill all the willow or something; that would make sense if the people depended on it for their living. And willow has a symbolic meaning too. It was once used by a man called Orpheus, who went into the underworld, the place of the dead. So it stands for the underworld, the world of spirits."

"Oooh, scary!" Sal's eyes went all wide and dramatic.

He laughed. "But it's also a simple healing herb. Long ago people used it as a painkiller. It was the first source of aspirin, you know—that and meadowsweet. Early man knew lots about herbs and stuff too. Did you know that?"

"No." Sal smiled. "I didn't. So . . . they used willow for healing and to make baskets and stuff?"

The owner gestured around him and smiled. "Take a look around you. See all those old baskets hanging on the wall up

there? All those wicker things were made locally. Peo
around here used to make baskets and chairs and cradles an
oh, *everything* you could possibly think of out of willow.
Everyone knew how to make things from the land back in the
olden days. Anyway, every thirty years there was a special summer solstice. And I know you're going to ask me why every
thirty years, so I'll save you the breath and tell you. The summer solstice happens in June. Now, how many days are there
in June, little lady?"

"Thirty!" said Sal. I could tell they both were enjoying this
enormously.

"Exactly. So thirty was a sacred number—"

"—because it was the length of the month of the sacred
solstice!" Sal finished.

"Exactly," he went on. "So every thirty years the people
who lived around here used to have a special solstice party.
They wove willow crowns, and they danced and sang to the
dying sun. Then, when the moon came up, they brought
meadowsweet flowers and lit willow torches and candles, and
the whole village would carry lanterns to an old stone circle.
The ceremony was called The Bringing of the Light. It must
have been important to the people who used to live here, for
it was passed down through the generations."

The Bringing of the Light, I repeated to myself. It made me
think of the verse on Eve's culvert stone:

Bring light again
To my stone pillow!

But Mr. Benjamin was speaking again.

"I know that they did all this at the stones at midnight. Old Jacob Everard told me that much."

"But where *were* the stones?" I asked.

He shook his head. "They were probably destroyed at some stage. Farmers and landowners often used to do things like that; they'd use the big stones for building and to make animal drinking troughs and the like."

I couldn't take my eyes off that wrinkled face with the closed eyes. I pointed up at her. "That face, is that the willow spirit?"

Mr. Benjamin swiveled around and looked up at the carved face. He chuckled.

"That? Bless me, no!" he said. Sal rolled her eyes at him to show how utterly stupid she thought I was.

"Well, who is it then, smarty pants?" I snapped at her. Behind his back, Sal quickly stuck her tongue out at me.

"That's the face of the village cunning woman," said Mr. Benjamin. "And I know you're going to ask what a cunning woman is, so I'll save you the breath and tell you. It's a sort of herb woman, a healer, what people used to call a witch. Her name was—"

He broke off and glared at me. "You're making a bit of a mess with those napkins, aren't you, lad?"

I looked down and realized I'd shredded our napkins into tiny pieces that were scattered all over the table. I scooped them up, embarrassed, and stuffed them into my pocket as he continued, turning very pointedly toward Sal and speaking just to her.

"*As* I was saying, the cunning woman was called Blind Meg, and she used to live right here in Sevenstone, down at Culvert Cottage. And some stay she still does. Some say that she still walks these parts."

His voice had dropped to a spooky whisper.

Sal and I exchanged glances. Culvert Cottage again! And now I knew the name of the old woman: B.M.—for Blind Meg. To my intense irritation, Sal veered right off the point.

"And this pub?" she whispered. "Is this pub haunted too?"

He nodded. "Oooh, yes. I was getting to that. It's haunted all right—by a man and a young boy. They sit together, muttering dark secrets. They sit right over there, in that window corner. If you turn around slowly, you might see them there, right now!"

We turned around. There sat Dad with Alfred, heads together, chatting.

"Oh!" said Sal with a yelp of laughter. "I thought you meant it! That's only my dad and your Alfred!"

135

"Is it? Your dad and my Alfred? And I thought we'd had a visitation!"

He laughed and winked and went to pour Dad another drink. He also brought us two sodas and put them down between us. "They're on the house," he said. "It's nice to see children so interested in history."

Sal took her drink and followed him back to Dad, but I drank mine in front of the fire, thinking of the druids. I imagined groups of people meeting every thirty years over the centuries. I imagined them watching the sun going down the latest it ever went down during the whole year. I saw them light their lanterns and torches and candles and walk in small, laughing groups over the fields to wherever the standing stones once stood. The light from their torches would flicker and dance as they approached that Iron Age monument. I didn't much like the thought of an ancient burial ground, stuffed with old bones. I'd had enough of the dead.

Sal came back and sat next to me. "Dad's having another drink with them," she said happily.

"Oh, no!" I groaned. I was desperate to get back, to continue my search.

She stared at me. "All this is really getting to you, isn't it?"

"So what?" I snapped back. "You're not being much help!"

"What! Who charmed all those meaty facts out of the owner? Not you, standing there scowling and fidgeting and *shredding* like some kind of giant hamster, that's for sure! Anyway, haven't you noticed something?"

"Yes. Your right braid is coming undone."

"Not me, stupid. The front doorway. Look what's carved all the way up its sides."

It was true. I hadn't noticed. Carved all the way up each side of the doorframe were many spears of small frothy flowers.

"They're the same flowers that Eve had on the stone culvert in the cottage!" she hissed. "Meadowsweet! And if a real live witch used to live in her house, then I bet she knows something about all this. And I'm going to find it out right now."

She pulled me over to where Dad was talking and said we were going for a quick walk. "Stay together," he muttered automatically, engrossed in something Alfred was saying about racing cars.

We hurried out and down the road to Culvert Cottage.

But Eve's front door stood closed and stayed closed, no matter how hard we knocked. From the depths of the house we heard both Phighdough dogs barking madly.

"They must be out," said Sal in a disappointed voice. "Come on."

As we walked away, I looked back and saw the front window curtain twitch.

Someone was inside the house but hadn't wanted to open the door to us. I felt a bit upset by this. Both Jacob and his daughter had seemed so friendly. Why would they be nice to us one day and unfriendly the next?

Dad stayed talking to the men for a long time. I kept grumbling about it until Sal got really angry with me.

"It's not as if he has many people to talk to, is it?" she said. "It's nice to see him talk and laugh with other men. You are so selfish!"

"I am not selfish! I just have a headache."

"Have a headache? You *are* a headache!"

We bickered a little more and then sat side by side, not talking to each other while we waited for Dad. All the time I longed to get back, to try to find Einstein or to investigate the hothouses, where Eve had mentioned the willow beds had ended. I figured that was where the willow crown might be leading me. I wanted to take a look at the carvings Eve had said were there. But as it was, when we finally got back, I found I couldn't get away at all.

Dad was in a much better mood, having offered Alfred that job. He was cheerful about the prospect of having more help and suggested we all have a card tournament before bed.

I smiled and played twenty-one, but all the time I was truly panicky about how to find out everything I needed to know. It was as if with every passing hour, the need to find the Seventh got bigger and bigger. I kept finding my thoughts wandering outside again—into the dark garden, tugged at by something old and horrible. I thought of all the statues there, standing in silence, their cold eyes staring into the darkness as if they could see through it to something I needed to see clearly too.

I played for a while, then said I was going for a shower, but they were still playing when I finished showering.

Desperate to get away, I paced my room. But the soft hum of Dad's and Sal's voices droned on and on. Every so often I'd go to the door and eavesdrop.

"Twist. Twist. Oh—bust!"

"Pay nineteen or over. Hard luck, Sal. You should have stuck at eighteen. I tell you every time."

They got quieter and quieter, and then—at last!—there was silence. I peered out. They both were asleep on the sofa, Sal nestled into Dad's shoulder.

The clock showed almost ten thirty. I got my flashlight, camera, and fleece, moving as quietly as I could. As I walked slowly, slowly, past the sofa, I spotted Dad's huge bunch of work keys on the table. What if the hothouses were locked? I picked the keys up, trying not to make them jangle. I'd have to make sure I wasn't seen this time.

CHAPTER TEN

T HE STAIRS WERE DIM and creaked as I snuck down them.
Rain shushed against the tiny turret windows. Great. Now
I'd get wet again, on top of everything else.

Just before I reached the hothouses, the tower clock in the
grounds struck the half hour. Half past ten. I hoped desperately
that Lord Minerva was snoozing over his nightcap brandy or, better still, already asleep. I hated the thought that he might be
watching me right now. What if one of his little console screens
flickered suddenly and there I was, tiptoeing toward the hothouse
doors? Even worse, what if Blind Meg herself was watching me?

I crept along, scared of every shadow, yet too scared to use
the flashlight unless I absolutely had to. The many panes of
glass of the main hothouse glistened with rain. Beyond them,
the interior was an eerie pitch black. I stole up to the door and
tried the handle. It was locked.

Quietly, I tried each key, holding my breath every time they jangled together on the ring. I remembered suddenly, just as the fourth key worked, that priceless black orchids were grown in these hothouses. Of course they'd be locked up each night! The lock clicked, and the door swung open.

The whole place smelled of damp peat and fungus. I stepped inside.

It was very ornate and tropical, a place for tourists to wander around and sit in and admire the rare plants and unusual trees and shrubs. It was decorated here and there with small fountains and carved stone water features. What was I looking for exactly? I was inching forward mostly by feel. I bumped into some kind of stone water feature and grazed my shin. It was no good. I'd have to use the flashlight.

In the strong beam the water feature I'd bumped into, a long stone trough, stood silent, its fountains and runnels switched off for the night. Its sides were richly carved. I spotted images of children, scores of children, dancing their way in and out among trees whose branches hung almost to the floor.

The beam from my flashlight moved on along the stone trough. Now I saw something that gave me a horrible start. It was a skull and crossbones.

It was carved above what looked like a small hill, with pointed frothy flowers all around. Under the small hillock there were more bones lying in a heap, hundreds of human bones and skulls, laid every which way.

All around it were clumps of young willow that people were collecting long switches of. Stone women stood weaving all manner of baskets and chairs and bags along the banks of a stone river. I stared at these tiny workers and nodded. This place was obviously steeped in willow history. But I didn't at all like the images of the skulls and bones. They were creepy and ominous.

I straightened up and went farther into the greenery. Tall palm trees, covered in creepers, stood everywhere. Exotic-looking shrubs were grouped tastefully together, with small pathways leading through them. Suddenly I stopped walking. I had found my statue.

It stood in a small arbor, silent and still, shining in the light from my flashlight. It was the color of pale butter: a finely carved model of a graceful girl, dancing. Her long hair was arranged in a huge braid that reached down to the hem of her dress. Her eyes stared back at me, blank and eerie. The foot of the statue was marked:

IN CHERISHED MEMORY OF OUR DAUGHTER

LADY ELLEN MINERVA

—NELLIE—

WHO DIED HERE ON THE SUMMER SOLSTICE 1886.

OUR HEARTS WILL NEVER MEND.

Once again there was something left at the base of the statue. I inched forward to take a photograph and gritted my teeth at the bright flash from my camera. Then I picked it up.

It was a small, pretty snow globe, the sort with a curved glass sphere set into a stand. Inside the sphere was water surrounding an ice scene of a little house covered in icicles. Its miniature window ledges dripped with icicles, and the roof was covered in snow. Tiny trees stood cold and frosted over. A little snowman stood there, and a robin on a twig in the foreground. It was old and very beautiful. But I didn't know where it might lead.

I slipped it into my pocket, glanced back at the door, and gasped.

Blind Meg stood outside the door, her wrinkled face pointing my way. Her eyes were shut, but there was an intensity about her, as if she were somehow observing my every move. How come this blind woman always knew where I was?

I blinked rapidly, willing the face to go away. But the next instant I saw the same face in another window, and then another, and still another. Everywhere I looked, in every single pane of glass, there was her face with its fixed concentration.

I spun around this way and that, not knowing where to turn. But there was no getting away from her. She was in every single windowpane, even the ones above my head. There were hundreds of images of her! I heard her voice, multiplied many times, whispering in the air all about me: "The Seventh! Find the Seventh. . . ."

I blinked, and all the faces and whispers were gone. Then I heard a new noise right behind me. I recognized it at once. It was a sound I'd heard Sal make many times while playing. It was the tap-tap-tapping of a small rubber ball bouncing on the floor.

My skin prickled with that familiar fear. *Turn around slowly*, I told myself. *There is someone in here with you.* The colors the flashlight picked out—the greens of the foliage, the deep colors of the tropical flowers, the reds of the tiled floor—all began to fade, to bleach to a sickly worm color. As they did, dread rose inside me.

My throat tightened with fear. I didn't want to watch another death. Why did I have to keep witnessing these awful things? It was as if each of the children, in trying to help me find my way toward the Seventh, was desperate to show me his or her own terrible story.

I turned around, and there, where the statue of her had been a moment before, was Nellie, dancing and skipping along, all her surroundings stone gray. She was dressed in a pale summer dress with short sleeves, and her silvery hair hung loose and free.

She was laughing as she ran along the path toward me, bouncing a small ball over and over. Then, almost as she reached me, she changed direction and began skipping backward. She skipped backward toward the door, trying to keep the ball bouncing as she counted. I heard her soft little voice coming from another century: "Sixty-five, sixty-six, sixty-seven . . ."

In a flash of dread I could see what was going to happen. She was so engrossed in her game, not looking where she was going. She was skipping backward—straight toward one of the long panes of window glass beside the door.

My heart leaped into my throat. Nellie bounced the ball a little closer to the floor to make it go faster, and all the time she skipped closer and closer to the pane of glass.

"Stop!" I tried to say. "Stop skipping!" But either I hadn't actually managed to get the words out or she couldn't hear me. She skipped and counted quicker and quicker. She was almost at the glass.

". . . seventy-five, seventy-six, seventy-seven . . ."

I hid my face, sickened, as she hit the pane of glass with a shocking crash. The splintering sound seemed to shatter the air all around.

Then everything grew quiet again, except for a steady drip-dripping of the tap by the door. I opened my eyes and let out the breath I'd been holding. But then the hothouse door suddenly shuddered and opened wide.

I was so terrified that I dropped the flashlight. The beam angled back across the floor tiles to the doorway. I gasped. Two feet stood there, brightly lit.

Two feet in fluffy pink slippers.

"Jim?" someone whispered.

It was Sal. It was only Sal! I went weak with relief. She ran over to me.

"Jim?" she whispered. "What are you *doing* in here?"

"I s-s-saw—I h-h-heard—" I was stuttering, stammering the words out.

She pulled me over to the door. "What? What did you see? What did you hear? Oh, come out, please!"

"A face at the windows—and at the door, and up there and *everywhere*! And then a girl, she was skipping backward, a girl with a ball . . ."

I stumbled against the door. It rattled loudly.

"Shh!" said Sally. "Be quiet—someone will hear you. It was only me at the door. It was *my* face, looking in. Come on!"

She dragged me out, her voice trying to stay soothing and calm. My legs didn't seem to work, but Sal shoved me along through the rain and back to the Hall. Just as we got to the side kitchen door, there came the low rumble of thunder. It echoed over the garden of statues and lit up the sky and lake briefly.

For a second as I glanced over Minerva's gardens, I saw the forms of the hundreds of statues lit by lightning. They were creepy and unmoving, yet I felt that at any moment every single statue would turn to look my way with blank, unseeing eyes, just as Blind Meg had done through the hundreds of panes of glass.

I stumbled with Sal through the kitchen door.

We rubbed ourselves dry with dish towels and shivered by the fire. Sal poured a glass of milk and microwaved it till it was warm. We shared it, huddled by the embers.

"Hurry up and drink it," she whispered. "We have to get back upstairs. We can't let Dad know—" She looked scared out of her wits.

"Why did you follow me?" I shivered.

"I woke up and saw you'd gone. I didn't want you to get caught; I was scared of Dad losing his job. Then I saw your flashlight in the hothouse and came after you. Now, give me that cup."

She carried it over to the dishwasher and put it inside, then glanced around to check that all was as we had found it.

"Come on—we'll talk upstairs," she whispered.

I opened my mouth to reply, then stood still. Sal hadn't heard it, but I had. A new sound had begun. It came from behind the internal kitchen door, the one that led into the main house.

It was the low whirring of an electric wheelchair. And it was getting nearer.

I stared at the door, my heart pounding. Sal heard the sound, opened the door to our spiral stairway, and quickly slipped through it. She whispered, "Jim, it's Lord Minerva. Pull yourself together. Come *on*!"

But I didn't have time to get to the turret doorway. The handle of the main door began to turn. I saw Sal's horrified face, and just before she shut the turret door, she whispered at me again. "Quick! Get under the tablecloth!"

I snapped out of my daze, ran to the table, and ducked under the long folds of its crisp white cloth. The wheelchair whirred its way in.

"Check that stairwell," I heard Lord Minerva say.

I heard the stairwell doorway being wrenched open and held my breath. Sal must have dashed out of sight just in time.

"He's not here, sir. Shall I go up there?"

"No. Go out to where you saw the flashlight. Check the hothouses. I'll wait here in case he comes back in."

Quick footsteps crossed into the side kitchen. The side garden door opened and closed. Everything was silent again in the kitchen. The wheelchair whirred into life and came closer, closer.

I tried to breathe as quietly as I could. I could just see, from the space under the tablecloth, the bottoms of the wheels as they passed and came to rest before the fire.

There was a long pause, broken by the rumble of thunder,

the flash of lightning. The fire crackled and hissed behind its guard. The fridge hummed. The side door reopened. The butler came in, clearly shaking the rain off. I heard the jangle of keys.

"There's no one there now, sir." He shivered. "But I found the main hothouse doors unlocked and these keys in them."

The keys! I'd forgotten Dad's keys!

"And are you quite sure it was the boy?"

"It was him, sir. The security tapes will bear me out."

I suddenly wondered if it might actually be *Einstein* they were talking about. Was he out there somewhere, plodding about? Did they now know he was playing truant? But Lord Minerva was speaking again.

"When we get back upstairs, get on the telephone to the gatehouse and tell Jonson to get his lazy backside out there to patrol the grounds. What's the point of having a gamekeeper if all he does is sleep and grow old?"

"I'll tell him, sir. I'll take care of it."

"Dead right you will. Just remember, Montague, your cozy retirement plan will vanish into thin air if anyone finds out about all this. There's already something important that's dis-. appeared, and you'd better find it *soon*, Montague! Do I make myself clear?"

"Quite clear, sir."

"Now get me back up to bed, and hurry up about it. It's far

too late at night for this sort of foolishness."

"Quite, sir."

The wheels whirred into life and faded away, through the door and back along the corridor.

CHAPTER ELEVEN

DAD STOOD BY MY BED, shaking me awake. He looked furious.

"Wake up! You've slept in—again," he said. "You're supposed to he helping me in the garden. Sit up! You look terrible. What on earth is the matter with you?"

"What? Nothing."

"Well, I want to know what's up, because something is. Sal thinks so too. I've just this minute been told you've been sneaking about again. Late at night. After you'd been expressly told not to! Why?"

My heart sank. Sal had snitched on me. A wave of cold fury swept over me.

"Never mind looking all sulky. *Why* do you keep sneaking off? Answer me!"

"I—I sometimes just need to be alone. To think."

"To think? Late at night?"

"Yes!" I almost yelled.

"In the dark? Why?"

"I like it then. No one bothers me."

"To think about what, for God's sake?"

I said the only thing I could think of.

"About—about Mom."

There was a long pause while he stared helplessly at me. Finally his shoulders slumped and his face sagged, as if the life had gone out of him all of a sudden.

"Well, you're clearly in no fit state to help me work, that's for sure. You'd better stay in here and try to catch up on some schoolwork; your last report wasn't exactly great. There's your old math book; you could work from that. You *promised* me you'd stop all this wandering, after what Lord Minerva said. You're risking my whole job here. You've let me down. You're grounded in your room until I tell you otherwise."

Panic filled me. I couldn't stay in my room all the time! I needed to be able to find the next statue, to try to figure out where the snow globe in my fleece pocket might be leading to!

"Dad, *please* don't ground me! I promise I won't go out at night again. Not ever. I *promise*, Dad!"

His eyes flashed angrily. "That's what you said before. Since I can't trust you, I'll have to ask Mrs. Benson to watch that you don't sneak back downstairs. You only have yourself to blame.

Now get yourself dressed and start work on that math. There's stuff for you to make a sandwich with in the living room."

I got dressed, my head screeching. It wasn't fair! Now I was banished to my awful tiny bedroom. I felt the whole world was against me.

I waited until Dad had gone and then I prowled the living room, grumbling aloud. I spotted Dad's old Minerva map—from the eighteenth century—and carried it to my room. I studied it closely, but I couldn't see anything there to help me. In the end I stuffed it into my bookcase and got out my old math book.

Boring, boring math. Who cared if the square of the stupid hypotenuse was equal to the sum of the stupid squares on the other two stupid sides?

But I did my best with it, working at the hated problems, page after page of them. How I wished Einstein were here to help me! He'd have these done in no time. So in an agony of math and frustration I wasted a day that dragged on endlessly, interrupted only by the boring liverwurst sandwich that I made for lunch. Time passed slowly.

Toward evening I turned a page and then looked up. I could hear water. Quite loud water.

Had it started to *pour* down now? I went to the window and saw that it *was* raining still—but not hard enough for these loud sounds. They were coming from . . . the small kitchen?

I opened the kitchen door, and a cascade of water ran out and over my feet. I gasped, horrified. Both taps were running, completely on, and the plug had been put in the sink. The water was flowing all over the floor.

I ran to turn the taps off. But the water sounds didn't stop. I realized there were *more* of them, this time from the tiny bathroom.

I ran to the bathroom door and saw that water—hot water, steaming water this time—was already seeping under it. Who had done this? Was it Sal, trying to get me into trouble? But I hadn't heard her come in.

I wrenched open the door, and a huge billow of steam rushed out to engulf me. The sink and the shower bath were overflowing. I rushed to turn the taps off and pull the plugs. Then I stood there, appalled at the mess. I heard Dad and Sal clatter in, Dad calling for me.

"Jim, are you there? I brought you a peace offering. Sal's made a wonderful meal! Where are—"

He stopped abruptly, and his mouth fell open as he surveyed the appalling mess. In his hands was a tray with what I presumed was my supper on it. I smelled the distinct scent of curry, and my stomach growled.

Dad exploded.

There was nothing I could say, nothing at all, to get him to believe me that it wasn't me.

"Of course it was you! You were just standing there at the bathroom door, for heaven's sakes, watching it all overflow!"

"It wasn't *me*!" I yelled again.

"Who else could it have been? There *was* only you here. Did you come up at all, Sally?"

Sal shook her head, her eyes wide. "No. I was too busy cooking with Mrs. B. Look, Jim, I've made my first curry."

"Which he will *not* eat," said Dad. "Not until he's gone down on his hands and knees and wiped up every drop of this water. Sally, go get some old towels from the laundry room. As many as you can carry. Go on—hurry up!"

Sal darted off. I stood there, yelling at him that it wasn't *me*!

"I'm tired of your lies!" he yelled back. "I want this cleaned up by the time I get back. I'd better go and see if the rooms underneath have flooded, see if it's gone through the ceiling. This is the very last thing I needed!"

He dashed off. Sal came back in with the towels. She plonked them down, glared at me, and flounced out. It was obvious she too thought I'd turned all the taps on, to pay Dad back for grounding me or something.

As I began to mop up all that water, I simply didn't know what I could do anymore. Everything seemed hopeless. The children had done this, of course, another stupid prank, like moving the flowerpots and—

155

Out of nowhere, something that Dad had said came back to me. Something about the old willow baskets. Something about water: "I just know there's something about willow that makes the locals think this valley is unlucky . . . something about the water changing."

As I mopped up, I had the growing sense that the children had turned the taps on not just to be mischievous, but to try to tell me something. Something about *water*.

By the time I'd finished, all the bath towels were filthy. My face was streaked with grime from this hideous, dusty old place. I wished I could just walk out and not ever look back.

Dad ordered me to clean my face up and then eat the curry in my bedroom. I didn't dare ask him if I could use the microwave, so I ate it cold. It was good.

Meanwhile, Dad and Sal were still cleaning the kitchen up. The water had seeped into the small cupboards by the sink and wet all the pots and pans there. Their soft voices came to me through the door, and as the evening wore on, Dad sounded less and less furious and more and more just plain tired. Sal always could calm him down.

I crept to my bedroom door and opened it a crack. I watched Sally wipe a cupboard dry. Dad was throwing some filthy towels into the laundry bin.

"It's lucky those rooms underneath aren't used anymore," Dad was saying. "If it'd been one of the collection rooms, it could have cost me a fortune. As it is, it's just an old classroom, and the water dripped down in only one corner. I hope no one'll notice. I can't tell Lord Minerva."

"He'd fire you, wouldn't he, if he found out?"

"You heard him the other night! He's angry enough as it is. I can't think what's got into Jim, I really can't. I'm going to have to keep him grounded until I can decide what to do. But how can I keep an eye on him, if I have to be out there working? He keeps sneaking off all the time!"

"I'll keep an eye on him, Dad. I can help Mrs. Benson in the kitchen *and* watch the door at the bottom of our stairs. I'd see him as soon as he came down them. I'll do it, don't worry."

There was a pause. Then Dad said quietly, "You're a good girl, Sal. Thanks. Good night now."

I saw Sal's delighted smile. "Night, Dad."

I closed the door and got into bed. Great. Now I had my little sister guarding me and my dad locking me up. Well, not locking me up exactly, but he might as well lock me up, setting Sneaky Sal to guard over me like this. Why did she pretend to be on my side one minute, then tell Dad on me the next? At that minute I hated her.

I'd forgotten to brush my teeth. I found Sal in the bathroom, brushing her hair.

"Don't glare at me like that!" I snapped.

"You've got to stop all this now," she replied through

clenched teeth. "It's all supposed to be some sort of game, right? But it's not funny anymore."

"But it never was a game, Sal—" I began, but she cut me short.

"But, but, but! Shut up with your *buts*!" said Sal. "You're scaring me and you're making Dad sick!"

"Dad? Sick? What do you mean, I'm making him sick?"

"Oh, no doubt you haven't even noticed the state he's in! You're too busy playing I spy up and down the place. He's walking around all gray and pinched and exhausted, just like he looked after Mom first went. I want you to stop this crazy game now. Right now. *Tonight*!"

"But, Sal, it's not a game, honestly!"

She threw her hairbrush at me with an explosive sound and flounced out. As I passed Dad in the living room on my way back to bed and said good night, he didn't even look up.

I woke up suddenly in the dead of night, shivering. My room was cold. My head ached. In the dark it felt as if cold hands were laying themselves upon me, shaking me gently. The chill from those hands needled deep into my skin and made it ache miserably.

"*Come with us!*" someone said.

Several voices. Children's voices.

"*Come with us!*" they said.

The freezing hands nudged me awake. I sat up and blinked into the darkness. Dazed, half asleep still, I went to the window and opened the curtains. A faint silver light shone in from outside. Clouds were rushing across the sky. A soft rain fell against the window, whispering.

"Come with us!"

I could hear the children but not see them—not quite. Just a few faint shadows stood around me. My hair stood up on end. I didn't want to go anywhere with dead children I could hear but not really see. I hurled myself back to bed and pulled the quilt over my head. But the hands came again, cold and insistent, nudging, pulling me to my feet.

"Come!"

I sensed then that they wouldn't let me disobey them— that they would never let me alone until I'd done what they'd asked. They pulled me and nudged me out of the room and onward. Down the spiral steps I crept, their icy hands never letting me go. I was shivering so much with fear that I had to clench my teeth to stop them from chattering.

One floor below our rooms, we stopped on the small landing. I was now facing the door that led out from the schoolroom corridor. Suddenly I knew where they were taking me.

Along the corridor they led me, until once again I stood before the tarnished brass plaque that said THE SCHOOLROOM. The door slowly opened without anyone's touching it.

The room was lit only by the dim reach of floodlights from the grounds. I could see straightaway the water damage that had been done earlier. A long patch of dampness blossomed out in a huge stain from the ceiling in one corner. In the wetness, the wallpaper that had been hanging off in strips had peeled off some more, at least another two feet. This was where the children directed me.

I saw some writing now visible on the plaster, something that had been covered up with old wallpaper for a long time. Now it had been revealed.

The writing was very small, penned in what looked like black ink. I read the ornate letters of its title, and my heart gave a huge leap of excitement. It said:

THE PROPHECY OF BLIND MEG, 1796

> *If the seven stones dishonored be,*
> *And slain the noble willow tree,*
> *Revenge will come each thirty year*
> *Till seven infant deaths bring fear.*
>
> *But if e'er the chain of seven br—*

The words stopped there. The wallpaper had pulled the next bit of plaster off the wall. It was a soggy mess, broken into many fragments, unreadable. I groaned, frustrated.

There came a crash that made me almost jump out of my skin. The windows had flown open. The curtains billowed out in the sudden breeze. I felt the icy fingers of the children touch my hands again as I was led over there.

Across the grounds the wind blew leaves all over the lawns. It was still raining. Every statue stood, glistening strangely in the floodlit night. Somewhere in the far wooded area a fox gave its wild cry.

"Look! Look!" the children whispered at my ears.

Then I saw it: a small movement on the path below. Out of the shadows came the tall, bent figure of the old woman. My blood ran cold.

She turned toward the house. The soft voices at my side had grown quiet. I watched as the hag began to raise one pointing hand. She slowly brought it up, higher, higher, until she was pointing directly at me. There was something terrible about this—a nonseeing person knowing exactly where I was. It felt all wrong, as if the different rules of two worlds were merging somehow: this world, where I stood, living and breathing at the window, and her world, the world of the spirits.

As I watched her, she seemed to begin to turn to smoke or fog. Wisps of moving gray rose up and regathered into a column of smoke that grew more dense. It rose and coiled my way. It found me standing there at the window. My vision clouded as it enveloped me. I felt as if I were being slowly encased in ice.

Something bitingly cold began to fill me, like the teeth of a gale from a polar place. My arms and legs turned heavy. Terror grew. The strange fog seemed filled with hidden things, things that a cunning woman, a witch, might know about, things I didn't want to know about.

I felt that nothing from my own world would ever work the right way again—not until I had done the thing I'd been asked to do. Not until I'd found the Seventh.

But I didn't know *how* to find the Seventh. The only Minerva child left now was Einstein, Lord Henry, who was playing truant. Was this all about preventing him from meeting death with a freak accident, as the other six had done?

As soon as I thought this, the window banged shut. The fog cleared. I sensed that the children had gone; I was alone in the dark schoolroom. When I peered out of the window, there was no one standing down there.

Somehow I found my way back to my room. I sat there, shivering with fear for the rest of the night. I felt different, filled with something that hadn't been there before. It was joyless and weighed on my shoulders as if some great dark bird had come to land on me and were sitting there. It stayed with me from that moment on.

CHAPTER TWELVE

ON THE MORNING OF solstice eve, I woke suddenly. I sat up in bed, puzzled to hear Mrs. Benson's voice rising and falling, then Sal giggling. It sounded as if they were in Sal's bedroom.

What was Mrs. B. doing up here? I wondered as I got dressed. Her small, wheezing laugh came to me, followed by a flurry of chatter from Sal. The sound made me feel excluded.

In the living room I found Dad's and Sal's blankets from the sofa, neatly folded, and Sal's bedroom door ajar. She and Mrs. B. were sitting at Sal's desk, heads together, writing on hundreds of what looked like jam pot labels. Mrs. B. was doing hers quickly and efficiently. Sal was decorating hers with colored sequins and glitter and felt-tip pens.

"Where's Dad?" I asked, stepping to the door.

They looked up. Mrs. B. regarded me for a moment.

"There's some toast and orange juice on the table," she said, "although I expect the toast will be like a piece of limp flannel by now. Rather you than me."

Sal held up her elaborate label. "SAL'S SPECIAL HAPPY BIRTHDAY JAM!" it said.

"I'm going to make some apple and ginger jam, Dad's favorite, for his birthday." She grinned.

"Dad's birthday?" I said. "But that's not till November!"

"Jam keeps," said Mrs. B.

I glanced across to the window. Still raining! I had to get going. I didn't have time to stop here and talk about jam, of all things.

"I'm not very hungry," I said as casually as I could. "I think I'll just go for a walk, stretch my legs."

Mrs. B. stood up, and several labels fluttered from her lap. "I'm very sorry, Jim, but I've been told to keep an eye on you. It's actually my day off. But I have to do all this labeling anyway, ready for next week's jam making, so I may as well do it up here. Your dad wants you to stay in your room and do some schoolwork—from the French book, he said."

My heart sank as I stared at the piles of labels: the ones already done, the vast amount still to do. Writing that many labels would take them most of the day for sure.

No. No! I couldn't be imprisoned here like this! Not when I suspected that Einstein was in danger! I objected as politely

164

as I could, but Mrs. B. firmly bustled me back into my room and handed me the orange juice, the flannel toast, and the French book.

"I'm afraid your dad is still very angry, Jim. All this wandering about, it has to stop! The master doesn't like it at all. Now sit in here and do as many of these exercises as you can. Then your dad might be a bit more pleased with you. All right?"

She was trying to be nice to me, I knew. But behind her words was the fact that she, like Dad, found me a major disappointment right now.

Sal was the good one. Sal was allowed to do what she wanted. Sal didn't need to be watched over like a baby. Sal wasn't worrying Dad. Sal was the best.

I sat on the bed and watched the door close behind Mrs. B. No one liked me. No one at all. I slammed the stupid French book across to the other side of the room. How could I get downstairs without their seeing me? What was I supposed to do, go rappelling down the outside of the dratted turret?

I could still hear them, working away in Sal's room with the door half open. From there they could easily see the only exit door. If I went anywhere near it, they'd see me for sure. Dejected, I sank back down onto my bed.

The only thing I could do was try to figure out what the snow globe meant. I got it out of my drawer and shook it. Tiny white flakes of snow swirled in a watery landscape. What was it trying to tell me? I decided to do a word chain to help me explore ideas.

Snow scene. Ornament. Toy. *Winter* toy. Christmas present? Snowman. Snowflakes. Cold. Ice. Freezing. Blizzard.

Robin. Branch. Dripping branch. Cottage. House. Icicles. Ice.

A thought began to stir. *Ice* and *house* seemed to pull at me. But I couldn't think what in the grounds the words might refer to. I went over to my bookshelf and pulled out Dad's old map, the eighteenth-century one.

My finger followed the lines of Minerva, from the gate-house and through the whole garden, past everything. Nothing even remotely sounding cold. So I traced my way toward the lesser-used parts, the outer boundaries where the old deer parks began. It took me a while to find it, a tiny building labeled ICEHOUSE.

Yes! This must be it, surely? I'd never heard of an icehouse. I went and grabbed the guidebook Mrs. B. had given me and flipped through it, hoping there would be something there to help me.

There was.

MINERVA'S ICEHOUSE

Icehouses were buildings used to store ice through the year. Minerva's icehouse is dug deep into the earth and was, each winter, packed with ice and snow. This was then insulated with sawdust or straw. The ice would remain frozen for many months, often until the following winter. It was used to keep summer deer kills fresh and was a source of ice for drinks, ice creams, and sorbets for Minerva's many summer balls and banquets.

I knew I was on the right track. The snow scene, with its teeny icicles and frozen house, was telling me to go to the ice-house.

As I thought this, a peculiar thing happened to me. I felt something stir deep in my belly. It was a dark thing, and it wasn't mine. I mean, I'd never felt it before, not ever. It's really hard to describe, but it was as if some dark thing within me had raised its old head and said Yes!

It might not make any sense to you, but this was the scariest thing that had happened to me so far. I thought of that gray mist Blind Meg had conjured up, the mist that had enveloped me, and I wondered if she had kind of taken over. It was a truly hideous thought.

I dashed back to the door, thinking hard how to get out. Mrs. B. and Sal could easily see the door to the spiral staircase. But they wouldn't be able to see much *else* of the room, I realized. So what else could they see? More to the point, what *couldn't* they see?

They wouldn't be able to see much of my bedroom door—just its hinged edge. So if I was careful, I might be able to open the door wide enough to sneak out and into the living room.

What else was in the living room? Was there anything that could help me? I tracked each item. The table—no good. The sideboard with its plates and cups and stuff—no good. The vacuum cleaner—useless. The dumbwaiter—

The dumbwaiter!

I saw it waiting there, the small traylike trolley that was once used to carry stuff from downstairs into rooms on all the floors.

I grabbed my flashlight and camera, carefully opened my door just enough to slip through it, then tiptoed across to where the small sliding panel stood closed.

"Then you get the jam going to a good rolling boil," Mrs. B. was saying to Sal.

"And how do you know when it's ready?" asked Sal as I slid the panel doors as noiselessly as I could to one side. Luckily, the tray was already at this floor, so at least I wouldn't have to winch it up.

"Oh, that's easy," said Mrs. B. from Sal's room. "When it coats the back of a spoon without slipping off, it's done."

I took a deep breath and climbed in, squashing myself into the horribly small space.

It smelled dusty and oily. The wooden tray creaked and

banged softly against the side of the shaft as I clambered into it. I cautiously knelt and slid the wooden doors closed again. Sal's voice became more muted.

"Mom used to make orange and ginger jam every Christmas," she said. "She used to write labels with me too, just like this. . . . Jim was never interested."

"No?" Mrs. B. replied. "What *is* he interested in? He seems like a strange boy to me."

"Oh, he is!" said Sal with great feeling.

I clicked my flashlight on and examined the oily chains. I would have to pull on these to lower myself down.

I reached up and gave a small experimental pull. The wooden tray I was crouching on shuddered but didn't move. I stared down at it uneasily. It looked strong, but what if it collapsed under my weight? Below me I could sense the depths of the house, all those floors yawning out under me.

I pulled the chains much harder. The tray moved down a surprisingly long way, about half a meter. I gave another tug and then stopped. Which other rooms would this dumbwaiter travel through, on its way down to the kitchen? What if someone in one of those rooms saw my flashlight through the cracks? They'd surely hear the little lift creaking past, but they'd be used to that sound. But if they saw an actual light in here, would they come to investigate?

I'd have to go down in the dark.

I gritted my teeth and turned off my flashlight. Everything became inky, except for a small crack of light coming through the tiny gap between the doors. Sal's chatter faded as I began to lower myself.

The small light from the sliding door above me got fainter and fainter. I thought of spiders, hundreds of spiders, and shuddered. I remembered the ghastly face of the old hag I'd seen in this very shaft. I almost panicked. *Keep calm, Jim, stop thinking about it!* I continued pulling on the chains.

After a while, around the sides of the tray, another sliver of light came inching into view below me. I pulled harder at the chains until the next door panel rose before my eyes. I must have gone down one whole floor.

I stopped here and pressed my ear to the panel. I heard nothing. I reached out, slid the panel a fraction to one side, and squinted out.

All I could see were furls of wallpaper hanging down and one edge of a desk. This was the schoolroom. I simply hadn't noticed the dumbwaiter in here before.

I continued downward again. The small light faded above me. Darkness returned.

I heard voices below me, men's voices. I handled the greasy chains as smoothly as I could as this new pencil of light came into view.

"But I looked, I did—for hours!" I heard an indignant

stranger's voice say. "It was raining almost too hard to see. I got wet through as it was. There was no one out there in the grounds at all!"

"I don't care if you almost drowned!" came a familiar mean voice. "I want you to do the same tonight. It's about time you earned your damned living."

It was Lord Minerva and, from the sounds of it, the game-keeper.

"But what am I looking *for*?" the gamekeeper asked.

"You know as well as I do there are prize koi carp in that lake and some magnificent sturgeon. Each carp alone is worth thousands of pounds, and there are at least sixty of them after the last restock. Why should I pay a decrepit gamekeeper who doesn't even watch out for damned poachers? Now get out there, and *stay vigilant!*"

"Very good, sir."

I heard the gamekeeper leave. But Lord M.'s wheelchair hadn't geared itself into life, so he was still sitting there as I drew level to the shaft.

I felt sick with fear. All my instincts told me to *stop moving toward him*, but this would appear unnatural, surely? As long as I kept moving as if someone were winching the dumbwaiter down in the normal way, I might not get discovered. Slowly and in an agony of nerves, I passed the door panel.

"Nasty little thief, sneaking about the place," I heard Lord

171

Minerva say as I approached and began to inch past. "I detest him and his ugly bucktoothed sister. If this carries on, my wonderful new head gardener will be looking for another job! Montague? Where the devil are you?"

"Yes, my Lord?"

"The new gardener told me that Busybody Benson is upstairs keeping an eye on the boy today—is that so? Who the devil is working the kitchens then?"

"The kitchen maids, sir," said his butler. "It's Cook's day off anyway, so there's a cold buffet on the menu tonight; the maids can manage. If you would care to glance at the menu, sir, I could take your order now. Would you prefer the ham salad or the cheese platter?"

"Neither. Salad is for rabbits, not people, and cheese is for mice. Order me some steak. Sirloin."

"But, sir, the doctor said—"

"The doctor is a blithering idiot. He charges too much, and besides, he has bad breath. I want peppered steak and fries— and *no damned salad!*"

"Very good, sir."

Their voices faded away again.

It got harder to pull the chains; my fingers were covered in oil and kept slipping. The cramped position was hurting my legs. I told myself just to keep going, mechanically lifting my arms up, grabbing the slippery chains, and pulling. Then soon,

soon, I would get out of here.

Just when I felt that my hands couldn't pull anymore, I saw below me the approaching gleam from the next sliding panel. I arrived with a small click at the paneled door.

I could hear the muffled sound of many people talking. I slid the panel a little to one side. Through the crack I saw the tail end of a group of tourists as they walked out of a huge ornate door.

I was in the Long Gallery.

From high up in the shaft, I heard a faint voice. Sal's. It came wailing and echoing down the chute, as if Sal now stood close to the doors of the dumbwaiter. "Jim, where *are* you, Jim?"

I struggled to slide my doors open. Sal would surely realize where I was and any minute now might look down the shaft. *Get out! Get out now!* But the panel door was jammed.

Far above me, a gleam of daylight suddenly appeared. Sal had opened the doors. I yanked the sliding panels aside, leaped out, and slammed the door closed again before the telltale light could tell Sal (and Mrs. B.) exactly which floor I was on.

I ran to the window, wiping the oil from my hands onto my fleece. There weren't many tourists outside; most of them must be in the gift shop or in the hall, staying out of the rain. I couldn't see Dad anywhere in immediate view either. I didn't even know where he'd be working. I'd have to be especially careful, indoors and out.

I avoided the Grand Stairway and found a smaller one that was all dingy. This part of the house was closed to tourists. I'd have a much better chance of not being seen.

The stairway led me down and came out somewhere behind the main kitchens. I could tell this from the nearby chattering and the clatter of pots and pans. The kitchen maids were arguing halfheartedly about who would scrub the pans and who would dry them.

I darted past, found a small exit, and walked out at last, free from the Hall. The paths were full of long puddles; the grass looked waterlogged. If only this rain would stop! I imagined Dad everywhere, expecting to bump into him around every corner. I was painfully aware too, as I made my way toward the back of the Hall, of the hated security cameras, fastened to trees or posts or the stone corners of the Hall.

Things were made even more complicated by the tourists, who weren't all indoors out of the rain at all, as I first thought. Some still trailed about with their guidebooks, huddled under huge MINERVA HALL umbrellas. These were big complimentary umbrellas stamped with red advertising. They were left in every location, to encourage people to stay even through the great British weather.

I had to dodge several groups before I finally reached the back of the estate. Here all the ornamental bits of garden were left behind. I was in dense, ancient woodland.

I kept going through it in the direction of the icehouse. I wished I'd picked up one of the umbrellas, but it was too late now. I was already wet through. The rain dripped loudly onto the leaves above my head. Unexpectedly, along came an elderly couple, squabbling in the sort of way elderly people do, idly, hardly listening to each other's replies. I ducked behind a tree as they passed.

"Hold the map a bit closer, can't you?" he said. "I've told you a hundred times now: I left my reading glasses on the hall table!"

"Oh, and that's my fault, is it?" she replied.

"Look, the Wildflower Garden is *that* way! We need to head backward past the house."

"I know. That's why I said precisely that. Ten minutes ago, if I remember correctly."

"Oh, let's give up. I'm drenched!" he suddenly said. "Shall we go for a cup of tea instead?"

"That's the most sensible thing you've said all day! The café's back this way. It *is*! Come on."

After their voices had faded away, I found the entrance to the icehouse.

It was half hidden in undergrowth, surrounded closely by very tall, old trees. The whole thing had been dug into a sloping bank, so that the entrance led underground. The doorway gaped, a stone-lined square that led into a tunnel filled with shadows. I didn't really want to go in there. I walked several times around it, trying to pluck up some courage. Near the entranceway lay a series of old stone troughs, now mossed over and thick with soggy leaves floating on a deep buildup of rainwater. I walked all around them, wondering what they had been for, and finally realized that they must have been filled with clean water every winter, to let freeze and stock the icehouse.

A tourist sign said:

WARNING

THIS AREA OF WILD WOODLAND HOLDS SOME RARE WILDFLOWERS. THIS IS THE ONLY PLACE LEFT IN MINERVA IN WHICH ONE OF THE ORIGINAL UNDERGROUND SPRINGS EMERGES BRIEFLY. THIS AREA IS PRONE TO FLOODING.

PLEASE DO NOT PICK THE FLOWERS.

ALL DOGS MUST BE KEPT ON LEASHES.

I remembered that at the bear pit too a warning had been given about rising water from underground, Once again I became aware that Minerva's water seemed important to all this. I stood peering nervously into the icehouse, and I imagined under my feet hidden watercourses, underground springs, running through Minerva like silver veins.

I couldn't delay the moment any longer. It was time to go in and find out why I had been led here. I stepped over a huge slab of stone, broken into two pieces, and realized it was the old stone door that once had blocked the icehouse. With a feeling of dread, I clicked on my flashlight and began to walk into the tunnel.

It smelled of earth and cold and a very strong animal smell—badgers maybe? It opened into a stone-clad square room. It was like being inside a tomb.

Something began to change. The back of my neck prickled. My mouth went dry with fear. It was happening again. The colors were fading. The beam from the flashlight became a sickly gray.

Already scared, I grabbed at the wall. I didn't want to witness any more deaths. My flesh began to creep, and I got goose bumps all over. I became cold, then more than cold. The room suddenly got much smaller. It seemed to suddenly be lined with thick blocks of ice, packed in sawdust. I was seeing the icehouse as it had been, in the past.

I heard footsteps running toward me. A little girl came storming into the icehouse as if she were filled with fury. It could only be Edwina, the next child on the list. She looked back at the entrance with blazing eyes. It was just a brightly lit square at the other end of the tunnel.

"See if I care!" she yelled. "If you won't let me come to your stupid solstice ball, then I shall keep away from you all!"

I heard men's voices from the woods. "Lady Edwina," they cried, "come back! Your mother is very displeased with you!"

There was no answer. Edwina ran into a shadowy corner and crouched down to hide. After a while the men outside gave up calling for her and came down the passageway, pushing a small handcart with squeaky wheels.

"Forget her," one of them said. "Spoiled little brat. I'm not hunting the whole woods—not while Cook's waiting for this ice."

They put gloves on their hands and lifted several smaller blocks of ice into the cart. For the larger blocks they used an enormous pair of metal ice tongs. They also heaved onto their shoulders what looked like a rib cage of some frozen animal. Edwina couldn't be seen in her dark corner, where she crouched, furious and sulking. They didn't seem to see me at all.

They pushed the cart back out and, with lots of grunting and shoving, pushed the heavy stone door shut. Just a slender crack of light spilled in from the edges of the door. Then the sound of their footsteps died away, the little handcart wheels squeaking as it moved away.

Edwina was huddled in a small ball of rage and tears. "Stupid party!" she yelled. "I hate you all!"

She had already begun to shiver. Her breath came out in a plume of condensation. It wasn't long before she ran to the thick stone door and beat her little fists against it. She began to shout for help, getting more and more hysterical as she realized she was trapped. She screamed for her mother. I stood there, horrified.

I didn't want to witness her terror. Her screams and sobs made me shudder. She was shivering violently. So was I. It was so cold in here—as cold as death. Then she fell quiet. I didn't want to watch her die. I could imagine it all: how her hair would slowly turn frosted, her lips blue with cold. I turned away, shaking.

As soon as I moved, the stillness of the icehouse began to take on outside sounds: the pattering rain, the harsh cry of a rook from the nearby tree. The entranceway was now a bright square again, lit with daylight.

I stumbled along it and staggered out, colder than I'd ever been in my life before. I leaned against a tree and tried to rub some warmth back into my hands and face. It seemed as if the marrow had frozen in my very bones. But the cold that gripped me wasn't just the cold anyone would get from that dark old place. It was a chill that came from long ago, the freezing grip of the ice that had slowly killed Lady Edwina and had finally become her tomb.

After a while I grew a little warmer. The rain was falling again, and I knew I was back in my own time, with the life of Minerva going on all around me. I sat down shakily on the edge of one of the stone troughs, and after a while I realized that just there, through the trees, I could see an ivy-clad statue.

I knew it would be hers. I walked over to it and saw Edwina's white marble face under the creepers of ivy. The never-ending life of the woods had slowly encased her, just as the cold had. Slender creepers decorated her dress like green embroidery. I didn't want to look into those dead stone eyes. I bent down and began to clear away the ivy and bindweed at the base of the statue until I could read the inscription.

LADY EDWINA FRANCES MINERVA
THIS STATUE IS ERECTED IN MEMORY OF A BELOVED
DAUGHTER AND SISTER,
WHO LOST HER LIFE IN THIS COLD PLACE,
SOLSTICE EVE, 1916

I remembered that there should be something left at the foot of this statue. I had to tear more bindweed away until I found what had been left.

It was a filigree hourglass, so tiny that it looked as if it might have come from a doll's house. Its glass bulbs were set in a tarnished metal stand that was engraved with a mother goose with her eggs. It was the sort of thing a small girl would love. Sal certainly would. I wasn't sure what it was supposed to signify. Cooking? Eggs? The kitchens perhaps?

But I didn't really have a clue.

I pocketed it, then spent a while picking flowers and carried them to the icehouse door. I laid them carefully at the entranceway, my heart aching. I thought of the children who had died in these grounds. Each child, it seemed, each in turn, wanted to show me how he or she had met death. Maybe it was hard to die. Maybe each one still couldn't quite believe what had happened and just needed to show someone, to invite someone in to share it, to feel a little less lost and alone. Maybe this was why I was seeing all these deaths. And after showing me, each child then left me something: a toy, a plaything, something of his or her own that nudged me on in this strange quest I'd been given. With each scene, I was getting closer to finding the Seventh. But none of this made the awful events of the past any easier to witness.

I walked back through the trees and out of that old woodland, gradually meeting the formal pathways again. Suddenly there was Einstein. He was plodding along, his shoulders hunched against the rain.

"Einstein," I said.

He stood still, not looking at me. I sensed that he knew far more about all this than he was telling me. But how could I get any information out of him? He wouldn't even look me in the eye.

He set off again. Cold, tensed up, wet through, and jarred

by all the awful things I'd seen, I ran after him and kept pace with him.

"It doesn't matter where you go, Einstein," I said. "I'll follow you. I want some answers. And I think you can give them to me. Where are you going?"

"This one is hiding," is all he would say.

"Yeah, I know." I sighed. "But where? Like I said, I'll just follow you."

So I did—right through the puddles that seemed to be joining up on the paths everywhere and all the way to the old stable block.

CHAPTER THIRTEEN

T HE STABLES DIDN'T LOOK particularly safe to go into. The
half doors of the stalls were either gone or hanging at a
slant. The roof looked dangerous, its tiles loose, its remaining
beams half rotted away. One section of tiles hung at a crazy
angle, as if the whole thing might fall down at any moment. I
stared at it uneasily and became aware that now I was almost
anticipating how Einstein might die. Tonight was the eve of the
thirtieth solstice. Was this what was going to happen to him?
Was he going to be buried under a roof fall? How could I stop
all this from happening?

He shoved open the half door of one stall, and I followed
him in.

Inside, everything was damp and decrepit. A saddle still
hung there, its leather covered with white mold. A manger
that once had been filled with hay stood rotting. The whole

back wall was thick with creepers that had somehow forced their way in. There was the sharp smell of mice or rats. The stone floor was almost totally covered with slanting lines of mathematical calculations drawn in chalk. Bits of chalk crunched underfoot. Einstein had obviously spent a lot of time in here.

"You're staying here?" I asked, horrified. "But . . . it's—it's *awful*!"

Einstein picked up a bit of chalk and began writing out a new sum. Back to his endless math problems. I had to get his attention somehow. I fished the child's hourglass out of my pocket and held it out.

"Look, Einstein. Do you know where this might lead?"

No reply. I tried again. "It counts something. You like counting, don't you?"

He regarded it solemnly for a moment, then spoke. "An hourglass, it counts time. An hourglass, it does not chime or tick; it is a silent counter of time. A sundial, it is even quieter. Shadows, they make even less sound than grains of sand falling. An hourglass, it might contain a million grains of sand, and they all change places randomly."

I considered his words. They didn't help much. He stared at his shoes again.

"Okay then, next question. What do you know about Blind Meg?"

"Blind Meg, she is a witch," he said instantly. "Culvert Cottage, it was her home. Witches, they still live there. Jacob Everard told me about Blind Meg. Blind Meg, she was a cunning woman and a prophet. Prophets, they know things that are going to happen."

From outside I heard someone yelling my name. It was Dad, and he sounded absolutely furious. I ran to the half door and peered over it cautiously. He was striding along the path that led to the stables, calling this way and that. What would I do if he came in?

I turned, terrified, to Einstein. "He mustn't find me here," I whispered. "Help me!"

"A person, he does not have to exit a stable block from the door only," he said.

I looked all around but couldn't see another way out. I ran to him. "Where? Where? How do I get out? Tell me!"

"A person, he might find a green window."

He pointed to the back wall, covered thickly in ivy. I ripped my way through the leaves. There was a small space behind it—a window, glassless.

Dad's voice came nearer. "James! Are you in there? You are in very serious trouble. You could have been killed in that dumbwaiter! Don't make me come in there!"

I scrambled up onto the small window ledge and hopped down the other side.

"Einstein!" I hissed his way. "Come on, get out, or my dad will see you!"

Einstein ignored me.

"Quick!" I whispered as Dad's footsteps came nearer. "Look, there's—there's a really interesting math problem here!"

His head came up. Interested, he climbed through the window and crouched beside me. From the stable I heard Dad shouting my name. Something crawled on my leg. An ant, then another, then another.

"I've had quite enough of this, James," Dad yelled. "Where are you?"

I held my breath. Ants swarmed all over my legs. I had to sit still. Moments passed. Dad strode away, swearing under his breath. I slapped at my legs, brushing the ants away.

"He's gone," I said to Einstein. "Come on."

But Einstein was busy staring at the crumbling wall. Ants swarmed in and out of what was obviously a nest.

"This one, he has counted seventeen going into the wall and twenty-four coming out. That is a total of forty-one ants. But if one comes back every two minutes, then it would take—"

I left him there counting, crashed my way through the creepers, and hurried toward the gatehouse. Some of the lower paths were now underwater. I ran splashing through them. I needed to see Jacob Everard.

He was half crazy, but I had to make him tell me whatever

he knew about Blind Meg and where I might find a complete copy of the thing titled "The Prophecy of Blind Meg, 1796."

The tourists were all gone. The only living things I saw were bedraggled peacocks, huddling in forlorn groups under the trees for shelter.

As I ran past the lake, I realized that I'd never really taken a good look at it. I was startled to see that the small central island was barely visible anymore. A few shrubs stood poking out of the surface of the lake instead. The water level was rising alarmingly quickly.

Off to one side, I could see, there was a weir, a strong stone structure. Water flowed over it whenever the lake level rose, and then vanished somewhere underground, toward the gatehouse, before flowing down to the village. The weir was roaring. Before all this rain, it never used to sound much more than a steady trickling, always there in the background. Now its loud roar scared me.

I could also see that farther around the lake there was a sluice gate, an extra overflow device. I hurried over to it. The whole contraption was the size of a car. It was a metal gate that could be raised or lowered by working a large lever at the side. This gate held back most of the water, letting just a trickle through its edges.

I could see that someone had pushed the lever down as far as it would go, to make the gate rise and let more water out, to cope with the extra rain. I spotted a huge boulder off to one side and went to stand on it, craning my neck to see what was beyond the iron gate. I could see a distinct channel gouged out of the land that sloped away and downhill.

This once would have eventually taken water to the sea. It was clear that in the past a far bigger, wider stream had gouged out this channel. The bottom of the channel now gushed with the steady water the sluice gate was allowing through. Clearly the overflow devices weren't enough to handle what was happening now.

Before I reached the gatehouse, I surveyed the incredible changes that were coming over the estate. Many of the smooth lawns were joined up by wide ribbons of water. It was an eerie scene. Stranded statues rose here and there. I could see a centaur streaming with rain. And a nymph up to her calves in water. Right by the gatehouse was a small cherub at ground level, the water already lapping at his marble lips, as if it were trying to drown him. When I glanced back, the lit windows of the Hall shone in reflection, the whole thing rippling here and there with strange new eddies.

I splashed my way down to the village under the dripping trees, hating my wet feet and the rushing, gurgling noises everywhere. The road was awash.

The village was a mess. The boggy area I'd got stuck in was now a deep pond. The frothy heads of the meadowsweet bobbed and drooped in the rain, barely above water.

Farther along at the Willow and Lantern pub, there were many cars parked all along the road, which surged with water. Every window was lit. I remembered what the owner had said about the solstice, with people coming from all over to gather. Well, it looked to me as if they'd all be stranded there.

There was no answer when I rang the bell at Culvert Cottage. But I heard both Phighdoughs barking loudly from the kitchen. I couldn't walk to the back without getting soaked; the path was under water. I banged on the front door and eventually yelled through the mail slot, "Eve! Eve! Please, I need to talk to you!"

The door suddenly opened, and Eve stood there, looking worn out and frazzled. "Jim, what on earth do you *want*? You shouldn't be out in this!"

"I have to talk to you. Please."

Eve glanced back over her shoulder and shook her head.

"I'm sorry, but Dad's having a terrible day. He's got himself all upset because of the flood. I'm trying to get him into his bed. Tomorrow."

"Tomorrow?"

"I'll talk to you tomorrow, I promise."

A huge crash came from behind her. "Oh, God! Look, I'll have to get some medication into him before he hurts himself."

She ran back down the corridor. The door shut but didn't

189

quite catch the lock and swung straight open again. I stepped inside and followed her into the kitchen. Jacob was standing there, wearing just an old undershirt and some even older underpants.

The dogs lurked under the table, their eyes nervous. Clearly they too were upset by the flood. Eve wrestled Jacob into a chair, trying to get a nightshirt over his head.

"Hello, young Jim!" bellowed Jacob with one arm sticking out of the neckhole. "Did you bring me any chips?"

"Er, no. Sorry."

"Oh, Dad!" muttered Eve. "The chip shop isn't open at this time, you know that. There's nothing open, just the pub, and you're certainly not going there. Now put your arm through here, and stop *fighting* me!"

The nightshirt was on at last. Jacob nodded knowingly across at me. "I know why you've come. It's all the flooding, isn't it?"

Eve picked up three pills and held them out, along with a cup of cold tea. She'd clearly been trying to get these pills into him for ages.

"Dad, stop talking and take these. Then you can play with your Rubik's Cube while I bandage my toe. You stood on it, and my toenail's bleeding. *Take them!*"

It was an order. Jacob swallowed them down, suddenly obedient. Eve threw him the Rubik's Cube to fiddle with. He stared at it angrily, as if he were sick of trying to work it out.

Eve meanwhile ran into the kitchen, her toenail oozing blood. The dogs ran forward and sniffed at it curiously. One of them tried to lick it better.

"Get away!" she yelled. "What are you, vampires? I'll catch rabies at this rate—on top of everything else!"

"Don't be absurd!" said Jacob in a suddenly lucid tone. "Rabies was eradicated from England long ago!"

Eve stood with her foot in the sink and rinsed her foot. She hopped about trying to dry it. "You'll have to go, I'm afraid, Jim. You're just overexciting him."

She hobbled to the stairs and up them. Here was my chance.

"Jacob, " I said, "what do you know about the seven stones? Can you tell me? Or about Blind Meg's prophecy? Or about the accidents that happened to the Minerva children?"

"They were no accidents!" mumbled Jacob to himself. "They was magic!" But I couldn't get him to say more, no matter how much I asked him, and soon Eve was back in.

"Have we any eels?" asked Jacob. "I could just eat a jellied eel."

"Dad, you've just eaten. I must find some socks or something; my feet are blue!"

"Blue?" asked Jacob, leaning out of his chair to see for himself. "Blue like the sky? Is that normal?"

She rolled her eyes. "Oh, for heaven's sakes! No one's feet are sky blue."

"Well, why on earth *say* it then?" he asked. "And they call *me* crazy!"

She went into the kitchen and began filling a hot-water bottle from the kettle. Jacob grabbed me and tugged me toward the parlor. He pointed toward the culvert stone.

The entire mantelshelf was covered in meadowsweet. There were flowers in jars, flowers in vases, flowers with their ends just wrapped in wet newspaper. There were at last fifty bunches of flowers there, and from the different ways they all were wrapped, I guessed they'd all come from different hands. The scent in the room made me feel giddy.

"Who brought all these?" I asked.

"People. Just villagers. Children. And some strangers too, people from the next valley and others from God knows where."

"Are these all for the thirtieth solstice?" I asked.

He nodded. "The flowers should go on the altar stone, but every year we put them here. Every thirty years we used to make the solstice crowns. But the altar stone is gone now."

Once again I read the words:

> *Betwixt the worlds*
> *Of life and death,*
> *Bring meadowsweet*
> *With its baby's breath.*

Bring candles bright
And rounds of willow.
Bring light again
To my stone pillow.

Eve bustled back in, wearing an old pair of men's slippers with holes in the toes.

"Hey! Those are my toe holes!" cried Jacob, pointing at her feet.

"Oh, Dad, you're driving me crazy. These are your old slippers from three years ago. Yours are on your *feet*. Are you still here, Jim? I really must ask you to go. His medicine will start to work in about twenty minutes, and I need to get him into bed before then. Dad, stay there while I see Jim out."

"I want my slippers!" cried Jacob. "I want my slippers! She won't give me my slippers! "

I was pushed to the front door. " Good-*bye*, Jim!" said Eve very firmly. "Another time. Tomorrow. Next week. Anytime. Just not *now*."

The door slammed in my face.

I stood there getting rained on for a few moments more. What now? I felt like giving up. Then I heard a funny knocking sound. It seemed to be coming from the flooded side path. I peered around the corner nervously.

A window stood open, the curtains billowing out crazily.

Jacob's grinning head stuck out of it. He beckoned me closer. He looked incredibly pleased with himself. I waded my way along the wet path.

"Quick, climb in!" He sniggered.

"You want me to *climb in*?"

"Quick!" He nodded. "Before my mother hears us."

I think he meant his daughter but didn't correct him. He helped me scramble in. I narrowly missed knocking over a yellow vase that stood on the windowsill but managed to catch it just in time. Jacob took it from me and replaced it tenderly on the sill.

"That was a wedding present!" he said, then put his finger to his lips. "Shh! Follow me—before those blasted pills start to work!"

He went to the door and opened it a crack.

"Follow you *where*?" I asked.

"To the cellar. There's some stuff I need to show you. It's about the Minerva prophecy. It's about this flood. Don't just stand there! Come on!"

I followed him along the hall and down a flight of steps into the tiny cellar of Culvert Cottage.

CHAPTER FOURTEEN

WATER HAD BEEN SEEPING into the cellar for hours. It was up to my knees. Jacob stepped into it, splashing as he went. He fumbled with some matches and lit a small candle that was standing there. Its flame reached out feebly.

"Brrr!" he said. "Why are my feet always so cold? She keeps stealing my slippers, that's why! I want my slippers back!"

His voice rose alarmingly as he sloshed, all agitated, back toward the cellar steps.

"Shh, Jacob," I hissed. "You're wearing your slippers—your *best* slippers. Look! Look at your feet!"

He raised one dripping foot and sighed with relief. "So I am. Well, how can she possibly have got them when they're on my feet? What a lot of nonsense she talks!"

"You were going to show me something?" I prodded him. I didn't like this. I wanted to hurry it along. Jacob was old and frail. He could get hypothermia down here.

"Was I?" he asked. "Oh, yes! Over here." He led me to several large wooden crates with damp cardboard boxes piled on top. He rummaged into the top box and took out several things. First, an old statue of the Eiffel Tower.

"Look! Look! This is from our honeymoon," he cried.

"Shh! Talk quieter. Or she'll hear you and—and then she'll come and—and *she'll steal your slippers again*!"

I felt awful saying it, but it was all I could think of under the circumstances. For an answer, he inspected both dripping feet and, in a relieved way, continued rummaging. He brought out a khaki uniform and stared at it in surprise. "Gracious! I never knew she'd kept this!"

"Jacob, please. Your medicine will start to work soon. We have to hurry! What is it you want to show me? About the *prophecy*?"

"Oh, yes . . . it's in here somewhere."

Out of the box he at last lifted an oblong package, wrapped up in the lacy folds of an old pink dress.

"My Gertrude wore this frock in Paris," he said. "Pretty, isn't it?"

"Oh, yes! Very," I said.

In fact it was falling apart and filthy. It stank of mold. He unfolded it carefully and brought out a thin browned book. The pages were curled up with age.

"What's this?" I asked.

"It's a book my mother used to have. It's very old. It's all about the night the lake was built. That was a big night for the bigwigs."

"The bigwigs?"

"Those wretched landowners. Take a look. You'll see!"

He went back to emptying the rest of the box. All was still quiet from upstairs. I carried the book over to the candle, opened it, and began to read it.

BLIND MEG AND HER PROPHECY

It was in the year of 1796 that the events surrounding Blind Meg occurred. Blind Meg was the village healing woman (sometimes called the cunning woman or the Witch of Sevenstone), who worked with herbs and potions and was a seer of all things hidden besides.

One day she received a vision. It foretold a set of dreadful events that were about to befall the village and darken Minerva forever, and it distressed her sorely. In secret she did write down her most important prophecy and entrust it to her brother, Isaac. He taught drawing skills to the Minerva children and was also decorating a ceiling in the new chapel that stands to this day in Minerva's fairgrounds.

Now, for some time Lord Bartholomew Minerva had looked about his lands and decided they were not serving him well. He wanted to build a forge in his village to make iron, for in the very next county a rival landowner had made his fortune in iron. He also wished for a carp lake, since the Benedictine monks of Rome had magnificent carp lakes built and Lord Bartholomew saw himself as grand and deserving of such riches as they.

Bartholomew planned to place a mill close to the village, in order to make good business use of the road there. Then, in the year of the thirtieth solstice, he did order the villagers to build an embankment upon his land, to eventually hold a lake that would feed his mill.

But the workers replied: "Never that valley, sire! For there stands our stone circle, and under it are the ancient bones of our ancestors, people who worshiped the water spirits and the sun and moon. Their tombs we shall not desecrate. There too lie the willow beds from which we make our living of basketry. Also in that valley are the seven pure springs, each one magical, from whose sacred banks our healing woman plucks her herbs. We dare not meddle with ancient magic."

Lord Bartholomew, knowing that he alone owned the workers' cottages and indeed the whole of that place, did reply heartlessly: "I care nothing for your superstitions! As for your healing woman, she gathers herbs for her secret potions, and some would call her a witch. Keep her away from me, and from now on there will be no super-stitious rites performed on my land!"

So the workers, scared to be turned out of house and home, began to build the embankment, along with a weir and a sluice gate to control the lake, and it all was ready by the special solstice.

THE BRINGING OF THE LIGHT

On the night of each thirtieth solstice the hamlet folk from miles about gathered for an ancient ceremony that was all their own. They were led by their healing woman, Blind Meg, as was their custom. Each girl wove a crown made of willow cut from the banks of Minerva's seven sacred springs. They brought rushlights and lanterns and all manner of candles in clay pots. So they danced their way at midnight to the place of the tomb, singing the ancient blessings to the seventh stone:

> Betwixt the worlds
> Of life and death,
> Bring meadowsweet
> With its baby's breath.
> Bring candles bright
> And rounds of willow.
> Bring light again
> To my stone pillow.

This blessing had been sung every thirtieth solstice for count-less generations, to appease the ancient willow spirits and water spirits that dwelt there. It is whispered that in pagan times the "life" that was offered had been that of a little child, instead of flame and leaf. Many a dark superstition about child sacrifice hung about that place, and folk lived in terror of angering the old spirits, fearful that they might once again claim the lives of children to appease them.

On that dreadful evening the workers laid down their tools and went with their families to the ceremony, so defying Lord Bartholomew. He had planned to close his new sluice gate the very next day; this would block the natural courses of the seven springs and flood the valley.

But that night Bartholomew and his lordly guests, seeing the defiant lights streaming upon Minerva Valley (and having drunk of much strong wine besides), did hasten as a pack to the Willow Vale. Without mercy they drove the revelers away with riding whips and stones. Then he and his guests together worked the lever, to close the sluice gate and trap the waters of the seven springs. Immediately the lake began to form.

THE HEALING WOMAN

Now to Blind Meg fell the sacred task of carrying the first candle of light to the ancient tomb and its seven stones. This was said to allow the dead to rest in harmony with the living and so demand the life from none.

On the eve of this particular thirtieth solstice, being very old, Blind Meg wished to pass her sacred work as healer on to her granddaughter. In Sevenstone, the office of cunning woman was held by her who wore a small stone charm, carved into the shape of a willow crown. Apprentice girls were

200

called herb daughters. As for the ancient stone charm of seven carved willow leaves, none knew its true origin, but all revered it.

At midnight Blind Meg was busy at the stone circle, beginning the ceremony of the Bringing of the Light. The whole village was there with her when the waters began to change. The seven sacred springs began to fill Willow Vale, far more rapidly than anyone anticipated. In the mayhem and panic of the rising waters, the village folk fled the valley, screaming, and they tried to drag Blind Meg over the embankment with them.

But she, knowing that the spirits had to be appeased, refused to leave until the ceremony was complete. Urgent word was sent to Bartholomew at the sluice gates that she still remained there. Inflamed with wine, he called her "witch" and "hag" and refused to halt his work. So just after midnight that ancient place was drowned in water, and she with it.

To this day the undercurrents of that woeful lake are deep and treacherous, and none dare enter them. It is said by some that the seven springs still fight to be free of that huge lake and so bring turmoil to the whole of Minerva Estate.

THE PROPHECY BLIND MEG ENTRUSTED
TO HER BROTHER

If the seven stones dishonored be,
And slain the noble willow tree,

Revenge will come each thirty year
Till seven infant deaths bring fear.

But if e'er the chain of seven break,
And there be no solstice child to take,
Then the lake will rise in that place of bone
And bring midnight death to Sevenstone.

These things are seen in ancient lore,
Yet Sightless Meg sees one thing more:
When the seventh child walks with the six
And seven flames burn seven wicks,
Then let the skytale tell a stranger
How he may prevent this mortal danger.

I sat there, shivering and wondering. The skytale again. How on earth did a painted ceiling come into all this?

Puzzled, I looked at the middle verse. What did it mean: *"if e'er the chain of seven break"*? Had Blind Meg meant that *unless* the seventh child died, the lake would rise to bring death to Sevenstone village? The prophecy terrified me. It seemed to be saying that one way or another, death was going to come. Even if I managed somehow to rescue Einstein from becoming the Seventh, people would die anyway in Sevenstone village. The lake would rise and presumably flood the whole village, bringing death.

I thought of the hidden waters and springs under Minerva and shivered. The weir at the lake had, not an hour before, been already roaring with too much water after all these long rains. I felt held in the grip of something huge and vast, something linked to the ancient spirits of willow and of water, who demanded to be appeased.

I thought I knew what a solstice child was: a child who was doomed to die on the solstice. I reread where it said, "When the seventh child walks with the six," and shuddered inside. If Einstein was the intended Seventh child, as he seemed to be, then the only way he could walk with the six dead children, the ghosts, was to die himself. And it all was about to happen tonight, on the eve of the solstice. There was even a big clue to when it all was due to happen: *"And bring midnight death."* That was the very time Blind Meg was drowned, on the eve of the thirtieth solstice long ago. I looked at my watch. It was nine twenty-five. I went cold inside to realize how little time Einstein had left.

"I have to go," I said suddenly to Jacob.

There was no reply. Jacob was sitting fast asleep, his chin upon his chest. His pills had obviously taken effect. I shook him but couldn't wake him. He was deeply asleep.

What now? I couldn't just leave him there, could I? I'd have to find a way to let Eve know he was there in the cold, wet cellar. I took the candle and climbed the cellar

203

steps. The house was silent.

I left the candlestick on the top stair and wedged the cellar door wide open. Eve would see the candle burning there right away. Then I ran back into Jacob's room and clambered out of the window, gritting my teeth against the freezing rain. Last of all, I reached back in and deliberately shoved the yellow vase off the windowsill.

"Sorry, Jacob," I muttered. "I know it was a wedding gift, but—"

It broke with a loud smash that brought Eve hurrying from the kitchen.

"What on earth?" I heard her say, and knew she'd seen the candle. Now she would go down and find Jacob there. Relieved, I set off, back to Minerva Hall.

The rain was driving down so hard that it was difficult to see clearly. All the way back, I tried to figure out where the hourglass might be leading. When I turned into Minerva's grounds, I gasped. Even in that short time the lake had overflowed shockingly. The weir roared horribly. In the air I could hear something new and strange, a low sound, like a vibration deep within the earth. It was as if huge waters were assembling underground and gathering force.

The words of Blind Meg's prophecy were coming true: The lake was rising. And if the lake rose up, the prophecy said that death would come to Sevenstone. It wasn't just Einstein in danger; it was the whole village!

I was scared by the strength of the water that surged everywhere. It sucked at my legs and threatened to pull me over. The lights from several stranded floodlights shone on the surface of the water, and still the rain pelted down.

Just then the nearby tower clock struck the three quarters. Quarter to ten! Dad would be furious with me for having run away and then staying out this late. In the back of my mind, something about the sound of the chiming clock tugged at me. It was something Einstein had said: "An hourglass, it does not chime or tick; it is a silent counter of time."

Time. Chime. Tick. Clock.

I stopped wading and stared at the clock tower. In a great surge of excitement, I suddenly knew where the hourglass had been leading me. The clock tower!

I struggled toward it and shouldered the heavy door open.

As soon as I stepped inside, all the outside sounds faded. Above me I heard a deep, slow ticking.

In one corner was a gloomy stairwell leading upward. This was barricaded by a chain from which a large sign hung:

DANGER! NO ENTRY!

On the bottom stair I found a flashlight and an old oil can. This must be what was used whenever the mechanism was cleaned. Unexpectedly, I heard a distant small voice, counting. It was coming from the stairwell—Einstein's voice.

"Einstein?" I called. "Are you up there?"

He counted on, ignoring me. I grabbed the flashlight, slipped my hand through the wrist strap, switched it on, and began to inch my way up the steps.

As I climbed, the ticking grew louder. The dimness, the closed-in feeling, the fusty air began to make me feel as if I were entering something eternally damp, like a tomb. Above me, the rain drummed down onto the roof.

I came to a small trapdoor that led upward. This opened into a room with a gaping circle in the center of the floor. The trapdoor banged shut behind me, making me jump. The sound echoed around the building. Nervously I edged closer to the central gap.

Hanging down into it were the frayed remains of five old bell ropes. Beside this hung an oily-looking chain and, finally, a fat metal rod with a black weight at the bottom—a pendulum that swung slowly from side to side.

I watched it swing to one side; a small metal claw slipped across onto a ratchet of a great wheel. *Tick*, said the clock. Then the pendulum swung back, and the little tooth slipped off its notch until the next tooth was caught. *Tock*, said the clock.

This was repeated over and over.

Even farther above hung the five bells, clustered together like strange bronze fruit. Einstein stood under them, counting the ticks and tocks.

"I wished you'd just *brought* me here, Einstein, when you knew the hourglass meant a clock."

No response. I tried again.

"Look," I said, "what have I come here to see? Is there a statue in here?"

He pointed to a small carving set into the wall. In simple letters, it said:

THE SEVEN SPRINGS BECAME THE ONE
AND FROM MINERVA IT DID RUN.

Seven again! I was sick and tired of seven! But at least this clue had led me to a bit more knowledge about the seven ancient springs. It seemed that at some point they all had run together to form one big stream. I thought of the wide channel I'd seen gouged out of the land behind the sluice gate and wondered if it could be there that the old waterways had run.

"The boy Thomas"—Einstein interrupted my thoughts — "he was killed by the bells."

"Killed by the bells? How come?"

"The bells, they used to be on long ropes pulled by men,

207

but now they are rung by a metal mechanism."

"Okay, but why are we here?"

He plodded to the small window and pointed down to the ground outside.

"The statue of the boy, it is down there. There are two hundred and twelve statues in the garden all together. Seventy of them they are in human form. Seventy pairs of feet add up to fourteen hundred fingers and toes, not including those of animals."

I stared down at the top of the stone head of the fifth child—Thomas—then turned back to Einstein.

"Look, Einstein, I've decided something. I'm going to tell Dad everything. I'm sorry, but I have no choice anymore. I just can't handle all this on my own anymore. All right?"

He didn't look upset. He just gave his funny little nod. From the clock came a sudden busy whirring. I was starting to feel dizzy and strange. It was as if—as if something were about to happen. A wave of nausea swept over me. All the colors around me began to fade. *No!* I thought. I didn't want to watch another child die.

"There are eight lace holes in each shoe," Einstein told his shoes. "That makes sixteen lace holes. If you multiply that number by itself, you get—"

He was interrupted by the bang of the trapdoor as it opened. Everything had smudged and turned gray. A thin, sickly-looking boy appeared at the top of the stairs, all out of breath.

I backed away. I saw the pale skin, the silvery hands that shimmered; and instantly the fear returned: the dry mouth, the thudding heart, the longing not to be seeing this at all.

He leaned against the wall as if the walk upstairs had exhausted him. His lips were twitching strangely. He didn't look healthy; he was small and very thin. He was incredibly out of breath. He let the trapdoor slam shut behind him.

"So. The forbidden clock tower at last!" he panted.

He sounded smug, as if he'd been wanting to get up here for ages and had only just managed to sneak in. He was looking all around, interested in the bells. Then the clock mechanism whirred and chortled and began to strike the hour.

My hands flew to cover my ears. It was *deafening!* The deep note seemed to reverberate through my entire body. My ears hurt, even with my hands covering them. It was the sort of noise that made your ears fill with intense pain. The bell tolled again and again.

Thomas, his hands to his ears, staggered to pry the trapdoor open. He was panicking too much to do it. His face began to twitch more and more. His breath got shorter and shorter, and then his whole body suddenly went stiff. He fell to the floor, twitching, and his eyes rolled back in his head.

I knew what this was. I'd seen someone at school like this. He was having a huge epileptic fit, brought on by panic and the earsplitting sound of the tolling bell. He foamed at the mouth and then suddenly went horribly limp.

All I could do now was protect my own ears. I knelt on the floor, bent double, trying to block the appalling sound.

The bell kept on tolling until it had struck twelve times. And I realized I was no longer in my time at all; I was witnessing all this in a scene from the past, when Thomas had died in here from epilepsy. At midnight, on a solstice eve long ago.

Finally, when the last toll died away, I opened my eyes.

Thomas was gone. The colors were returning to normal again. Einstein stood staring at the bells in awe. I grabbed him, wrenched the trapdoor open, and ran down the stairs, pulling him along.

As I opened the door, water came gushing in. I waded through it, my ears still hurting. Einstein followed me just as a huge crack of thunder erupted overhead. I yelled out in fright. All my nerves felt stretched to the breaking point; seeing each death scene was draining something out of me, emptying me somehow of all my strength. I just didn't want any more of all this. I wanted it to stop now. The clock, I noticed as I blinked into the rain, showed several minutes past ten.

I waded over to the statue we'd seen from way up there. Rain fell all over the stone Thomas in silver sheets. He was just as I'd seen him, thin and puny-looking, with the same curly hair that ran throughout the Minerva family. This statue showed him sitting on a stone bench, smiling faintly. I read the inscription.

THIS STATUE WAS ERECTED
IN LOVING MEMORIAM OF THOMAS LOUIS MINERVA,
WHO LOST HIS LIFE HERE,
SUMMER SOLSTICE EVE 1946

The statue stood up to its knees in water that was flowing in a rapid stream toward the lake. In the crook of his stone hand a small toy was wedged. A tiny boat. I picked it up and pocketed it. Another clue. I was exhausted, sick and tired of not knowing what was best to do.

"Come on, Einstein," I said. "It's time to go back to the Hall. You'll get into trouble for playing truant, but I can't help that. I'll get in loads of trouble too, so at least you're not on your own."

"This one, he likes being on his own," he said.

"I know you do. Come on—if you follow me upstairs and wait in my bedroom, I'll go find my dad. He'll know what to do."

There was no one in the living room, but as I led Einstein into my bedroom, I heard the sound of sobbing coming from Sal's room. Einstein walked over to my books and began to count them. I put the toy boat down on the bed.

211

"Stay here," I said. "I'll be back in a minute. All right?"

He gave a brief nod, so I left him standing there and went and knocked on Sal's door.

She sat in a crumpled heap, sobbing great, loud sobs that Mrs. Benson, aghast, was trying to hush and comfort. Dad stood nearby, a shocked expression on his white face.

"What's happened?" I asked.

Dad looked at me wearily. He didn't look angry at all. He just gave me a long, tired look that wrenched my heart, then went to stand by the window. That look was filled with such disappointment that it made me want to cry.

"You're wet through," he said in a dull voice. "I've looked all over for you."

"What's up?" I asked.

"What's up? What's up?" screamed Sal furiously. "Your stupid sneaking about has ruined everything. I *told* you to stop it! I *told* you it was important! Here—read this, you selfish, selfish *pig!*"

She hurled a crumpled letter my way. I picked it up off the floor and read it.

Minerva Hall

Dear Mr. Brown,

    I regret to inform you that since you could not as requested keep your children under control, I have no choice but to terminate your employment. Your son has been caught on several security tapes, trespassing at all hours of the day and night. The latest tape showed him leaving the grounds earlier—after he had been expressly forbidden to. This continued disobedience will no longer be tolerated.

Since this employment brings its own living accommodation, I have taken the liberty of booking you all into a bed-and-breakfast in the nearest main town, starting from tomorrow. The cost of this will be taken from wages already owed to you. This arrangement should give you ample time to find other work and housing. Since your employment was on a trial basis, I trust that you find this fair under the circumstances.

I shall of course supply references for any future employment, in which I shall not necessarily mention the shocking behavior of your son, depending on your cooperation with my own decision and wishes now.

Minerva

I let the letter fall. Sal burst into fresh tears. Mrs. B. put her arms around her and gave me a disgusted glare.

Dad had lost his job.

He had *lost* his job! He had lost his brand-new start in this new place, meant to help him get over Mom's death. And it was all my fault. I'd ruined everything.

But it wasn't fair! Lord Minerva was trying to hide something here and was getting rid of Dad just to stop me from finding it out. As soon as Dad heard everything I had to tell him, and met Einstein and everything, surely he would understand. He'd see how I'd had *no choice* but to disobey, because of all these weird things that had happened, because people were in danger. And the lake was still rising. If it overflowed the weir, it would flow straight down to the village: a huge volume of water, fast-moving and deadly. If the village was flooded already, it would be absolutely treacherous if the entire lake overflowed. Oh, he would see how it all had been.

"Dad. I've brought someone to meet you. He's in my room. It's Henry, Lord Minerva's son. He's in trouble. I was going to tell you all about it. It's why I kept sneaking off—"

Mrs. Benson was staring at me with her mouth open. An indignant look came into her face. "You horrible little boy!" she exploded. "Lord Henry isn't in your room at all! Montague and the master drove him to London themselves not ten days ago!"

Dad turned around and folded his arms. Sal was so angry, it even stopped her from crying.

"But he *is* here, Dad!" I cried. I began pulling him toward my room. "He didn't really go to school. He played truant. He's been hiding out in the stables. Just come and *look*."

We reached my door. Sal and Mrs. B. followed. I flung the

door open. Einstein stood exactly where I'd left him, his hair dripping wet. He looked suddenly very shy to see all these people. "There!" I pointed in triumph.

They looked into the room, then turned to me, eyes blazing.

"Liar!" yelled Sal. "How could you do such a thing to Dad? I hate you!"

"It's wicked to hurt your poor father like this," said Mrs. B. in a voice shaking with rage. Dad just looked too angry to even speak.

"What? *Look*, Dad, this is Einstein."

"Einstein!" exclaimed Mrs. B. "The master's son is called *Henry*, you stupid child!"

"I *mean* Henry. Henry, tell them. Don't ignore me again— not now! Tell them about the children . . . and the standing stones . . . and the old hag. Tell them!"

"Twelve books, there are in this room," he told them. "They are mostly encyclopedias. But that one, it is a book on mathematics. On its cover it has a calculation showing the Fibonacci sequence."

"*Tell* them!" I cried, desperate.

Dad spoke in a terrible voice. "It's bad enough that you've been so disobedient. It's bad enough you've lost me my job. But to play tricks like this at such a time!"

"You pig!" screamed Sal, running to Dad's side and grabbing his hand. "I'll never speak to you again as long as I live!"

"But-but . . ." I was stammering, staring from face to face, bewildered.

"Stop it!" yelled Sal. "Stop pretending there's a boy here. You know perfectly well that the only boy here is *you*!"

My mouth dropped open. I stared at Einstein, then back to them.

"What? He's standing right there!" I was almost in tears of frustration.

"That's enough!" roared Dad. "You will stay in your room until I tell you, do you hear me? You will not go anywhere at all—not anywhere, from this minute onward. I am so *tired* of you!"

He strode out of the room. Einstein immediately followed him. Mrs. B. and Sal gave me the filthiest of looks and walked out, slamming the door behind them.

There was a long pause during which my mind struggled to comprehend. Then understanding crashed into my thinking and made my legs buckle. I sank down to sit on the bed.

They couldn't see Einstein. Only I could see Einstein. I wasn't supposed to rescue him from danger at all. Einstein was already dead.

CHAPTER FIFTEEN

ORROR FILLED ME. I put my head in my hands and felt as if my brain were exploding. My thoughts flitted backward and forward, all kinds of things occurring to me, one after the other.

Something clicked into place. That security tape that had filmed me at the village church. It had shown a tiny me, running out of the side door, and the angry priest running after, vestments billowing out. It had shown just me, I realized now, not Einstein, who was running by my side. Too scared at having been found out, I just hadn't registered this at the time.

And poor Dad. Poor, broken Dad. The very idea of that sly creep, Lord Minerva, getting the better of him made me grit my teeth and swear under my breath. How *dare* he? Dad was worth ten of him and his butler put together.

I'd been wrong about so many things. Like "find the

Seventh." It's true that I'd figured out that the Seventh must be Einstein and that Einstein was Lord Henry. But how could I possibly have found him if I didn't even know he had died? I didn't even know *how* he died. The last clue, the one Thomas had left, was a toy boat. Still in my pocket. I took it out.

I suddenly remembered that in the small graveyard, one gravestone had given details of the child's death. Beatrice's. "Drowned." And it was pretty obvious where she'd drowned. The same place the toy boat was leading me toward: the lake. Yet I didn't know what to do there!

In the next room Sal's sobs had subsided at last. The only sound was that never-ending rain drumming at the window. I tried to figure out what I might have missed, something to help me know what to do now. I racked my brains, realizing there were less than two hours left now until midnight of the thirtieth solstice. What had I missed? What was my task, if it wasn't to prevent Einstein's death? "Find the Seventh." Was I looking for his *body*? Everyone thought he was at school—but I knew different!

I reached into my fleece pocket and pulled out the soggy booklet Jacob had given me. I read its prophecy through again, trying to interpret it line by line.

If the seven stones dishonored be,
And slain the noble willow tree . . .

This was obvious now that I knew the history. If the stones were flooded by greedy Lord Minerva, it would kill all the willow beds.

> Revenge will come each thirty year
> Till seven infant deaths bring fear.

Seven deaths had been prophesied. Einstein was the seventh.

> But if e'er the chain of seven break,
> And there be no solstice child to take,
> Then the lake will rise in that place of bone
> And bring midnight death to Sevenstone.

It all began to click into place, one piece after another. Because Einstein must have already *died* before the sacred eve of the thirtieth solstice, there was no Minerva child for the vengeful spirits of the burial mound to take. So they were cheated out of their seventh child, whose death on that night had been decreed so long ago.

I read it through once more, saying it aloud to myself.

THE PROPHECY BLIND MEG ENTRUSTED
TO HER BROTHER

> If the seven stones dishonored be,
> And slain the noble willow tree,

Revenge will come each thirty year
Till seven infant deaths bring fear.

But if e'er the chain of seven break,
And there be no solstice child to take,
Then the lake will rise in that place of bone
And bring midnight death to Sevenstone.

These things are seen in ancient lore,
Yet Sightless Meg sees one thing more:
When the seventh child walks with the six
And seven flames burn seven wicks,
Then let the skytale tell a stranger
How he may prevent this mortal danger.

I thought back to that night at the schoolroom window, when Blind Meg had raised her hand and pointed straight at me. I remembered that awful mist that had come my way from her, as if she was filling me, was taking over me in some way. Now I saw her inside my head, her eyes closed, her hair wild. She whispered old answers to my thoughts, helping me.

I suddenly saw things with her inner knowledge. I understood that Lord Bartholomew's greed had drowned the seven stones—had "dishonored" them—and that the ancient spirits of that sacred place had become angry. They had no longer been satisfied to accept an offering of fire, to bring light to their dark world and bridge the gap between the living and the dead. Nor could they be placated with meadowsweet, the healing flower in that area. The spirits had demanded instead seven deaths, all from Lord Bartholomew's descendants. Seven children's deaths—one for each of the sacred stones.

Yet the prophecy said that if this chain of seven deaths ever got broken "and there be no solstice child to take," then the lake would rise and "bring midnight death to Sevenstone."

This was why the flood was happening, Blind Meg made me see. Because Einstein (the "seventh child") was *already dead*, the solstice ritual of the exchange of life could not now be performed. So the very ancient spirits of water and willow were angry again. The old waterways were going to rise up, all seven of them, and claim life from the village instead.

And then Blind Meg disappeared from my thoughts as suddenly as she had appeared. I felt inside me an old strength, a knowing of hidden things. I understood far more about the comings and goings of the ghosts of Minerva Hall. And I wondered now if Blind Meg was the evil hag I'd assumed after all. She was certainly terrifying, but maybe she was just an herb woman, trying to appease the spirits still? Had she just been trying to help me all along?

"The old one is watching you," she had said. I'd thought *she* was the old one. But what if she had meant something far older had been watching me? The ancient spirit of that sacred place?

I went back to the prophecy.

> These things are seen in ancient lore,
> Yet Sightless Meg sees one thing more:
> When the seventh child walks with the six
> And seven flames burn seven wicks,
> Then let the skytale tell a stranger
> How he may prevent this mortal danger.

The seventh child, Einstein, presumably did walk with the six! He was a ghost too, a dead child, like all the others. I wasn't sure, still, how seven flames and seven wicks might come into it all, but one thing I was sure of was this: The only part that hadn't happened was the bit about the skytale. The prophecy said that the skytale could somehow teach a stranger something, and prevent this "mortal danger."

What if I was that stranger? If so, maybe there *was* something more I could do to prevent all this destruction and death. Maybe *this* was my real task. If Blind Meg had seen, long ago, that this was possible, then surely I had to at least try! A skytale.

I reread the word, but I still couldn't understand how a painted ceiling in an old chapel could possibly help me now. Once again that old, insistent knowledge seeped back into me. It seemed to focus all my attention on the word *skytale*. It suddenly

222

struck me that in the prophecy, it was spelled as one word, not two: *Skytale*, not *sky tale*.

Could it be that . . . well, that the word *skytale* had a different meaning from the one I'd thought it meant?

I ran to the row of encyclopedias and pulled out the volume for subjects beginning with *S*. Excitedly, I flicked through the pages. The next minute I was staring down at the page with shock.

This is what it said:

SKYTALE or SKITALE *(pronounced to rhyme with ITALY, as if it were spelled skit-ally).* A skytale is the earliest form of code. In the fifth century B.C., the Spartans used a system of code consisting of a thin ribbon of papyrus wrapped around a staff. When a person wanted to send a message in secret, he would write it along the length of the staff so that when the papyrus was unwrapped, the message would be unreadable. To read it, the recipient would have to rewrap the papyrus strip around an identical stick. Only then would the letters line up.

This was the illustration:

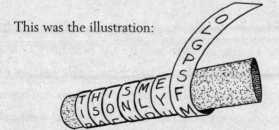

My heart began to race as I thought back to the first time I'd ever seen the word "skytale," on the wall of the schoolroom, alongside that drawing of the domed ceiling and the candlestick.

There had been *two* things in the drawing all along, two things! The skytale was not the painted ceiling at all. *It was the giant candlestick!*

I was astounded. I had taken wrong turnings so many times. I thought back to the faded ribbon, with the letters running all along it, that held up the tapestry. This must be the thing that could be wrapped around the candlestick, just as papyrus could be wrapped around a staff. More facts slipped into place.

Blind Meg had written her prophecy and entrusted it to her brother, Isaac. He, the booklet told me, was an art teacher, *who was decorating the chapel at Minerva*. Isaac was teaching art to Lord Bartholomew's children at the time. So he would have had plenty of opportunity to draw this clue on the schoolroom wall, perhaps hoping that some later pupil would be able to unravel it.

I got the sudden feeling that Blind Meg had *instructed* her brother to do all this, in order to leave the possibility that all this evil could be undone. But he hadn't been able to leave her prophecy at Minerva openly in view of Lord Bartholomew, who was such an enemy. After all, Bartholomew had heartlessly allowed Blind Meg to die. He could just as easily be a danger to her brother if he suspected he was writing things down about the truth of what had happened. So Blind Meg had come up with a *hidden* way to reveal the truth, so that someone, "a stranger," might be able to find her message.

I was that stranger. I suddenly knew it, deep inside.

I knew I had to go back to the chapel, to learn whatever the skytale might be able to tell me. I checked my watch and groaned. All this figuring out and reading and the stuff with Dad and Einstein had taken almost another hour. There were now only sixty-five minutes left to midnight.

I quickly changed into dry clothes and then hesitated again. I desperately wanted to see Dad before I went out again into the dangerous water. I wanted to try to apologize, to try to explain, to somehow make him feel better.

Before I could change my mind, I went to tap softly on his door. There was no sign of Sal; she must have cried herself to sleep.

"Yes?" came Dad's weary voice.

He was sitting on his bed with them all spread out in front of him: Mom's photographs. They were scattered about an empty suitcase with a pile of tangled clothes next to it. He looked at me through red-rimmed eyes.

"Dad, I'm sorry. I'm so sorry."

It was all I could think of to say.

Dad looked toward the window for a moment. Eventually he spoke. All the energy seemed to have gone out of him.

"Still raining!" He sighed. "Will it ever stop? The ford will be more than flooded. I was worried sick when they said you'd gone out. I'm at a loss for why you did this. . . ."

He rubbed at his hair until it stuck out in all directions. I just stood there fidgeting until he looked my way again and spoke. "I expect you're wondering how I'm ever going to punish you. Is that it?"

I shook my head. No! I hadn't come in here because I was worried about myself!

"The funny thing is, Jim," he said, "I can't seem to bring myself to be angry anymore. I just feel tired. I don't blame you. Not really. I blame myself."

"You—you blame yourself?"

"Yes. I should have known this new start wouldn't work. I'm not very good at all this, am I? I never seem to know where my children are half the time. It's true, what Alicia said: I'm never *with* you. Not really."

Mrs. B. had said that?

Dad picked up a sweater, began folding it, then stuffed it into the suitcase. One arm stuck out awkwardly. He took the whole thing out and tried to refold it. It was just as bad the second time.

"Look at the state of that!" he said. "I never was any good

at packing, was I? Your mom used to say I packed a suitcase like a toddler chucking toys into a toy box! I might have known I wouldn't be much without her."

He put the photo down and smiled weakly across at me. "You'd better pack too, Jim. Tell Sally as well. We'll try again somewhere else. We'll all try again. Tomorrow."

He turned his back and went on packing. I walked out of the room and went back to my room. I closed the door, but from the outside, not the inside. This was just in case Dad was listening. There were tears running down my face, but I rubbed them away.

It was now or never.

I walked into the corridor and down the stairs. No one saw me leave the turret or the Hall. As I stepped into the flooded gardens, there came a long flicker of lightning that lit up the whole scene.

There were barely any sections of lawn left now. Water flowed and gurgled downhill toward the lake. I waded into it up to my thighs, and its force was appalling. It was all I could do to stay on my feet.

Something soft floated by and brushed against me, making me leap out of my skin. It was one of the Minerva peacocks. It was dead. Its beautiful tail trailed behind it, all its magnificence gone.

I hoped desperately that in the whole of Minerva and

Sevenstone, this peacock would be the only thing to die tonight.

Outside the chapel each little gravestone now stood protruding from the water. I imagined the cold water seeping down and down, into the old earth and mingling with the bones of the children and their pets. I shoved the thought away.

The door was far harder to open than before; water stood behind it as well as in front of it. I had to work to shoulder it open.

My flashlight lit up an eerie scene. The entire chapel was under several feet of water. The row of pews rose like a strange brown hedge in a silver lawn that moved and rippled. The whole place dripped and echoed.

I waded toward the tapestry. The bottom of its hem was under water. The water seeped upward as if the tapestry were a wide wick. All the lower colors were bleeding together, the gentle willows losing their sharpness. I stood on a pew and lifted the tapestry down. It was easy to unhook the ribbon.

I was watched silently by those gods and goddesses painted above my head. Their sightless eyes stared at me and made my flesh creep.

I stepped carefully from bench to bench so as to stay out of the water. I was so cold. My feet were numb. I put the ribbon around my neck while I heaved the heavy candlestick dripping onto the bench. Then I tipped it onto its side and inspected its long tall stem.

I suddenly remembered that Einstein had described the letters in here as flat but needing to be curly. I smiled. He knew all about the skytale that rhymes with *Italy*. He was a genius; he'd probably worked it out long ago, loving the cleverness of it, not caring at all about what it meant. He just knew the strip of letters had to be curled around the candlestick.

I glanced down at the letters on the strip. It didn't look like anything much.

It took me a while to figure out how to do it all and where to begin. At the top of the candlestick, just under its drip tray, was a small slot in the metal, and another was farther down. This candlestick had been custom made for this job! Clever old Isaac.

I wound the ribbon on. The meaningless letters began to rearrange themselves in this form of ancient code. This is what it looked like:

My heart began to beat fast as the message emerged. The hyphens, I soon saw, showed word breaks.

This is what it said:

> IF GREED FOR IRON ENTOMBS THE STONE
> THEN ONLY IRON CAN ATONE
> LET STONE BE RAISED ALOFT AND BREAK
> THE IRON THAT ENTOMBED THE LAKE
> THEN YOUNG AND OLD CAN COME TO GREET
> THE WILLOW FAIR THE MEADOWSWEET

I read it over and over. "Greed for iron" obviously referred to Lord Bartholomew's wish to get even richer from iron. He had insisted on making a forge near the village because other men were making their fortunes in the new industry, iron smelting.

"The iron that entombed the lake"—I wondered about this. Could it mean the iron sluice gate that held all the water back? It must be!

I checked my watch. It was twenty minutes to midnight!

I jumped down into the freezing water and waded out of the chapel. The water swirled everywhere, its currents tugging at me like many small hands.

CHAPTER SIXTEEN

T HE WIND GOT WILDER and colder. The storm cracked and
flashed overhead. I made my way to the lake, which had
flooded acres and acres of land by now. Only the curve of the
embankment, built so long ago, was holding the water back.

The weir sounded hideously, dangerously loud. I skirted
around, trying to stay on higher ground as much as I could,
until I stood by it.

The water was surging over it too fast, way more than it
had ever been built for. It poured over the weir stones but
couldn't drain away fast enough underground, as it was
designed to do. I could feel a thundering vibration under my
feet, as if the land would split right open at any moment. I
watched the small rowboat that was moored nearby buck and
strain at its ropes.

The force of all this water was dreadful. It was too much

for me. Terror gripped me and made me shake inside. What did I think I could do against such force? I was weak, puny, just one boy. I could do nothing. All I wanted to do was run back to the house and hide. Doubts crashed everywhere inside my head. Why had I ever thought I could help Einstein or the valley or anyone? I was helpless and scared. I wanted Dad. I began to turn away.

Instantly a huge bolt of lightning flashed and crackled overhead. It lit up something standing on the surface of the water—someone old and bent. My stomach turned over.

Blind Meg stood there, her eyes closed, her hair wild all around her head. Her feet stood on the water as if it were solid. She began to walk toward me. Fear engulfed me.

I tried to move, to run away, but couldn't. My arms and legs seemed to have turned to stone. I watched her come nearer. Five paces away. Four. Three. Two. One.

She reached for my arm. Her ice-cold hands grabbed me and began to pull me back with her, toward the water. I stumbled and fell into the shallows, and still she pulled. The water got deeper and deeper. Then there was no lake bed under my feet anymore, and I was engulfed.

Blind Meg had me! She was pulling me toward the center of the lake, deeper and deeper. Yet she had tried to help me— hadn't she? Hand't she? I tried to scream, but no sound came out, and water filled my mouth. I held my breath as we went rapidly down toward the dark lake bed.

My lungs began to hurt with the need to breathe. A steady beat began in my head and neck, the beat of my pulse. Then it seemed that I heard words, keeping time with it, all around me:

> Betwixt the worlds
> Of life and death . . .

I heard the tribal beat of drums in my ears and the simpler beat of running feet. I felt as if I were stuck in some terrible in-between place, a place where the skin between the world of life and the world of death was getting thinner.

A terrible cold flowed from Blind Meg's hand into mine. It was an iciness that came from beyond the grave. Then my need for breath got too much to bear.

I began to struggle and fight and kick and do anything I could to get away. But she was far stronger than I was. The pressure built up unbearably in my head and made my ears ring. She dragged me farther down, until the floor of the lake loomed into view.

Through the dim water I watched as we approached large black shapes. They were tall, jutting out of the lake bed. The blood roared in my ears as I registered that there were seven of them.

Seven stones.

She had dragged me down to the stone circle.

It shimmered through the dappled water. It was silted round with many years of mud and dirt. I felt my body land in this soft bed of silt and begin to sink into it. It sucked at my legs, as if dark, flabby hands were holding me.

Something changed. Now the sound of laughter and of chatter came close—the voices of many young people who had visited this place over the centuries. A sweet strong scent came to me: the scent of meadowsweet and the fresh green leaves of the willow. I was surrounded by the voices of many long-ago young, strong people. I could hear voices, singing a blessing in this place, as they had always done:

> Betwixt the worlds
> Of life and death,
> Bring meadowsweet
> With its baby's breath.
> Bring candles bright
> And rounds of willow.
> Bring light again
> To my stone pillow.

Blind Meg tugged me until I was held over the central stone, the sacrificial stone. Now I was about to die here too.

234

Neon sparks appeared behind my eyes. *I had to breathe! I had to breathe!* I couldn't bear it anymore.

I exhaled a huge bubble of air, and water flooded into my mouth and up my nose. It hit the inside of my head like something solid, like roots of lead or steel, rushing in to fill all the tiny capillaries and veins and tubes that I was made of.

Then I was floating in the electric yellow light that was filling my head. And still I was held tight—until suddenly everything became dimmer. The pain in my chest eased, then vanished.

Time seemed to slow down. Before me, I saw, the hag was quite at home here under the water. Her thin finger pointed to something on the lake bed. There was something lying by the center stone, wedged there in the silt: a small mound, a muddy bulk. I looked closer at it.

There was a jacket. Trousers. A thin hand, bloated purple and mottled.

I saw the soles of a pair of boots—two legs. Intertwined with these were the links of a huge old chain. It was a body weighed down by chains. I knew who it was at once.

At last. I'd found the Seventh.

My mind began to drift.

I gazed at the body dreamily. I found that if this was Einstein, I didn't mind much anymore. If this was what it was like to drown, I didn't really care after all. It was quite pleasant. Quite

235

calm. I closed my eyes. All I wanted to do was sleep.

Let me sleep.

A cold, unwelcome jolt ran through me. Blind Meg began to pull me upward.

Upward? I thought dreamily. Was she pulling me upward?

The lake bed with its seven stones faded into the distance. Ahead, the surface loomed nearer: a dappled silver, moonlit. It came whooshing toward me.

I burst out into the clean air and inhaled at last. Water came up through my nose and mouth. I vomited. The currents of the water were strong, but someone far stronger lifted me and helped me to the side of the lake. Blind Meg was helping me toward the shore. Under my hands I felt solid ground. I clutched it and spluttered. I felt myself being laid down on the soggy ground beside the weir.

I lay there, retching and gasping, trying to get my breath back. The image of that body lying there under the tons of water seemed etched on the backs of my eyes. As I heaved and gasped and spat muddy water out, I understood all at once why Blind Meg wanted me to drain the lake. It only then that the body of my friend could truly be found.

But something new was happening. Under my hands I could feel that rumbling, dangerous vibration growing, as if the ground were just about to disintegrate. Nearby, I saw the long

236

line of stone monks, the statues that followed each other on stone-sandaled feet. They seemed to be wading through the water, their white hands clasped. The water around their knees seemed to quiver, as if that vibration underground was growing stronger.

There came a great crack nearby. I turned to see a massive oak tree hit by lightning. Its leafy top exploded into sparks of fire. The fire surged down its trunk. The tree began to fall toward me, its roots unable to keep hold of the earth.

I forced my weak limbs to move, to scramble to one side. The huge tree trunk fell, hitting the weir with a sickening crash. I saw part of the weir break and start to crumble. The shuddering water seemed to lift its voice as it struggled to burst free. The whole weir was about to give way. *And all this water, the whole lake, would flow down to the village, destroying everything in its path!*

I splashed and waded out as fast as I could around to the other side of the sluice gate. Its thick iron was buckling with the weight of water slamming into it. The flow surged and foamed, trying to escape through the small gap under the gate. In a flash of lightning, my eye was drawn to something on the ground nearby. It was the pale boulder I'd stood on earlier tonight when trying to see over the sluice gate.

As soon as I saw this stone, words filled the air: the hidden words from the Skytale.

IF GREED FOR IRON ENTOMBS THE STONE
THEN ONLY IRON CAN ATONE
LET STONE BE RAISED ALOFT AND BREAK
THE IRON THAT ENTOMBED THE LAKE
THEN YOUNG AND OLD CAN COME TO GREET
THE WILLOW FAIR THE MEADOWSWEET

From the land itself, a strange power seemed to rise as if sparked into life. Strength filled my body. My arms tingled and ached and itched. My eyes were fixed on the boulder. I knew I couldn't possibly lift such a heavy thing. Yet something else was bringing me strength.

Faintly, in the background, I heard the clock tower bell begin to strike twelve. Hurry! Hurry!

I ran forward and bent to grasp the boulder in my arms. The trembling of the ground under me seemed to rise and build. Its sound filled my ears. Images began to flash before my eyes: images of green fronds, of flowing hair that was made of willow, of a huge, strong face whose skin was willow bark. I glimpsed a vast arc that was made up only of willow, that stretched from one side of Minerva to the other, a swath of something young and green. I felt on my face a breeze from a time long gone. It brought a whispering, the soft sound of dry leaves moving against leaves, of boughs growing in strength.

Something ancient was rousing itself, was rising with all its power. Its strength flooded into me. I began to lift.

The boulder didn't want to let go of the land. It was hard to dislodge. But more strength came, and then the huge boulder was rising, higher and higher. It was raised all the way above my head until I felt its vast weight bear down on me. My arms trembled and ached. Pains shot down my shoulders, but still that old strength came from Minerva's land, where willow beds once had grown. There came a pause as if the whole world were holding its breath.

Then I hurled the boulder onto the metal sluice gate.

It hit it with a mighty reverberation that filled the air. The iron buckled and folded like thin cardboard. The next instant the entire iron gate was swallowed by the surge of water that poured in a mad torrent through the gap. The lever was ripped from its mechanism and swept away. Even the struts the gate had sat in vanished.

The water reared up, racing free of the land, away from the crumbling weir that threatened to flood the village. It surged and swelled in its rush to escape Minerva. It gushed toward my feet.

I ran to higher ground, grabbed at a tree trunk, and hid my face from the roar and the smash of it all. Water, cold and strong, swirled around my feet. I clung tighter and cowered under the thunder and lightning that erupted above me.

I stayed like this for a long time, for what seemed like

hours. It was as if both the earth and the sky were being swept away together and there was nothing I could do but cling on and wait as the lake emptied itself at last into the old channels the water had once flowed in, away from Minerva and from the village, across the fields toward the waiting sea. . . .

The storm was leaving. I stood up shakily and let go of the tree trunk. I was still standing in water, but now it had no deathly strength. It was easier to stand in. The row of stone monks was scattered, some lying on their faces, some lopsided, some broken in two. Distant voices came, shouting from the brightly lit Hall. The grounds shimmered with reflections.

I suddenly saw that a floodlight was attached to the tree, behind my back. A softer rain fell sparkling toward it. Lightning flickered still in the distance, its thunder getting fainter and fainter.

I stood in front of the security light and waved toward the voices.

My shadow waved too. It stretched like a giant across the floodwaters of Minerva.

CHAPTER SEVENTEEN

T HAT NIGHT I SLEPT as if I hadn't slept for a hundred years. When I awoke, Sal was sitting there, fully dressed. She picked up a cup of lukewarm cocoa.

"Can you sit up?"

I sat up and sipped it gratefully. My throat felt parched and sore, as if I'd swallowed nettles or something. I winced and touched my head. A slow throbbing was behind my eyes.

"My head hurts," I said.

"And no wonder!" said Sal. "You almost drowned, and you have a huge bump on your head. Feel it—just there. It's like a duck egg! You might have concussion. You've got to tell us if you have a headache, feel sick or faint, and all that. Do you?"

"Not really." I lied; I didn't want any fuss.

"After they picked you up from near the lake, you passed out. You were delirious, rambling on and on about a witch and a

241

body under the lake. Dad was worried sick. The doctor couldn't get here. The ford was impassable; the roads were awash with water. The entire sluice gate collapsed, and all the land just beyond it. The lake burst its banks and flooded fields for seven miles. But it missed the village." Sal took a breath at last.

"Has anyone been hurt?"

Sal shook her head. "Don't think so. Anyway, in the end Dad gave you a quarter of a sleeping pill to shut you up. You've slept ever since."

Sleeping pill? That explained it. I felt as if my whole body were twice as heavy as it usually was.

"Where is he?"

I was so tired. My arms and legs were sore. Everything was sore.

"Dad? He's in the main kitchen. He said we could go down when you woke up if you feel up to it. Do you?"

I said yes. But it took me forever to get dressed—every single muscle hurt—so Sal had to help me, and while she was doing this, she yakked on and on about it all. Finally I asked her what the grounds looked like now. She took me to the window.

"See for yourself," she said.

The rain had stopped at last. A feeble sun shone glistening on all the mud. The grounds looked like a war zone. Fallen trees lay uprooted. Leaves and twigs covered what had once been the grand lawns. Shrubs and bushes were uprooted and lay thick with debris and silt.

Black mud was everywhere, with flowerpots and urns and half-broken statues rising out of it. Statues lay on their faces in the mud.

Stretching from the kitchen garden to the remains of the lake were wide wooden boards laid over the mud. At the end of this wooden pathway, a small group of men moved to and fro at the standing stones. The lake itself was just a vast black scar of mire and puddles. There was a small shallow pond left in the base, and jutting out of it were the seven stones.

"Well, you found the stone circle all right!" said Sal.

"The whole lake . . . gone?" I whispered.

"Yes. And that's not all. The thing you were rambling about? The body under the lake? Well, they found one," she whispered. "A body in the lake! Look—those men are the police and a forensic team and an archaeologist. There are hundreds of ancient bones down there too, apparently from the burial cairn! Jim—how did you *know* there was a body down there?"

I shrugged.

"I can't explain," I said. "But—who found the body?" (Apart from me, I meant.)

Sal grinned with relish. "One of the kitchen maids, coming back in to work. The roads are just about passable now. She splashed her way over the grounds, saw the body, and screamed like a stuck pig. Or a stuck peacock."

"Have all the peacocks died?"

"No. Just a few. They can climb and hop pretty well, Dad said. Are you ready to go down?"

I nodded.

"I'm cold. And hungry," I said.

In the main kitchen, Mrs. B. was bustling about, pouring broth into flasks. Two kitchen maids stood at the sink, eyes agog with gossip about the body.

Dad turned from a huge pan he was lifting to the stove for Mrs. B., looked up, and saw me. He walked over and gave me a huge hug. "Jim," he said simply.

"I'm sorry, Dad." I wasn't sure what I was apologizing for. For disobeying him. For losing him his job. For nearly drowning. For worrying him.

But he shook his head. "None of that's important," he said. "It's only important that you're here. Now."

His eyes were grim and exhausted.

Mrs. B. came up with a steaming bowl of chicken soup. She gave me a quick, fierce hug. "Eat it!" she said before bustling off again.

I sat down and spooned it in obediently, with Dad and Sal watching me all the time. They stared at me as if I'd returned to them from the dead.

In a way I suppose I had.

After I'd eaten, we were just sitting, smiling at each other, when the main door swung open. In came Lord Minerva, his wheelchair whirring its way through the busy kitchen. The kitchen staff all stood to one side to let him pass. A police officer stood on each side of him, with Montague behind.

His nibs sat there and pointed at me. "That's him," he said. "James Brown. He's been caught on the security tapes, trespassing, many a time. Then only last night he was seen on one of the tapes, running toward the sluice gate. I don't know what he did, but I know he was involved. Every single one of my prize carp have died."

His face was filled with a look of deep hatred.

The police officer nodded my way and smiled thinly. I got the feeling he had been in Lord Minerva's company too long and was weary of him.

"I'm Inspector Bedford," he said. "You must be Jim. Let's all go into the side kitchen, shall we? Come on—it's a bit more private in here. Now, Jim, are you feeling better?"

"The body in the lake," I said, "it's Einstein."

Everyone looked at me as if I were crazy, but I shook my head.

"I don't mean *that* Einstein, I don't mean the physicist. I mean Henry, Lord Minerva's son. He's all wrapped in chains."

Bedford stared at me. He took Dad to one side. "Beats me

how he knows about the chains," I heard him mutter. "We haven't released any details yet."

I became quiet again. I couldn't explain anything.

Lord Minerva was white. He gave an explosive snort. "My son, indeed! Whatever next? The boy is a proven liar!"

Mrs. B. spoke up. Her eyes were bewildered as she spoke to Inspector Bedford. "Lord Minerva and Montague here told me they had driven Henry to school themselves," she said.

Lord Minerva threw her a bitter, baleful glare. "You must have been mistaken, woman," he said. "I said that we had driven him to the *train station*. We put him on a *train* to school."

Mrs. B. colored until she was red in the face. "You know very well that Henry was terrified of loud noises. No one could get him into a train, not even me. He certainly would never have let *you*!"

"Nevertheless, he did let me."

"Inspector," she asked in a tight voice, "is the body . . . well, is it of a young boy?"

His eyes were sad. He seemed to be trying not to answer the question.

"There is a lot of silt on the corpse; forensics haven't finished yet. The body is facedown. All we've recovered so far are the boots. Would you like to sit down, Mrs. Benson?"

She nodded and sagged into the chair he brought her.

A corpse. Einstein was a corpse.

"Are they brown boots, with light blue laces?" she asked faintly.

"They are," he said gently.

Mrs. B. went white. "I bought those boots not three weeks ago," she said, "for Lord Henry. Three weeks ago. They're sent for by mail order. They made a mistake with the color. They sent brown instead of black. Henry hates brown. He's always hated brown! He only likes black or bright colors, the color of crayons or chalk."

At this my heart gave a great lurch.

The butler, I suddenly noticed, looked as if he might at any minute be sick. Lord Minerva meanwhile just fixed Mrs. Benson with a mean stare.

"That body is *not* Henry!" he snarled.

Mrs. B.'s eyes flashed angrily. "Well, it's easy enough to find out," she told Inspector Bedford. "Look in his boot!"

"His boot?"

"Yes! Look in his boot! He always something in his left boot. It was an old key."

"A key? To where?" The inspector looked bewildered.

"He wouldn't tell me that. But I know he used to call it the cat key."

"Cat key? What on earth is a cat key?" asked the inspector, but Mrs. B. shook her head.

Meanwhile, something nudged at me, far in the back of my mind. A small, insistent noise I'd once heard in the corridor of our turret. An insistent sound, over and over, of a cat crying, "Me! Me! Me!"

But Mrs. B. was speaking again. "I never questioned him about it. The poor little boy had to have something all of his own. I just know he'd found the key somewhere upstairs years ago."

The inspector nodded to his colleague, who slipped out of the room for a while. Meanwhile, something else was dawning on me.

"That was why he always walked in that funny, plodding way," I whispered. "*Because he kept something inside his boot.*"

Mrs. B. turned to me, a strange look on her face. "How did you know he walked like that? You never met him, surely?"

"Um, I—I just knew. I don't know how."

She stared at me closely, as did Dad and Sal. I knew they all were remembering when I'd taken them to my bedroom to let Dad meet Einstein.

"Oh, my good lord!" said Dad softly. He sat down suddenly.

The other officer returned and handed something over to Inspector Bedford. He examined it for a moment, then held it up. It was a key. Mrs. B. burst into uncontrollable sobs.

Something else slipped into place. "I think I know where that key is for," I said slowly. "The locked room. The locked room in our turret. Its door is all sealed up."

"There he goes again!" exploded Lord Minerva. "More lies. More rubbish! What locked room?"

Inspector Bedford stepped toward Lord Minerva. "If you don't mind humoring me, sir, I'd rather just check it out."

Dad gave me a long, careful look and then spoke. "I know which room he means," he said. "Follow me."

Up the spiral stairway we went: Sal, Mrs. B., and I.

As for Minerva, the inspector insisted on his coming too, he and the butler. They took the elevator to the floor below, and then there was a lot of shoving and pulling to get him up the final stairs. All the way up, he got angrier and angrier with everyone until he was red in the face. But eventually we all arrived outside the door of the locked room.

Dad examined it closely.

"It's *well* painted over," he said. "Years and years of paint. Look, the edges are thick with the stuff!"

"Well, I'm not surprised," said Mrs. B. "That room certainly hasn't been opened in all the time I've worked here."

"Any particular reason why not?" asked the inspector.

Mrs. B looked uneasy. "We were all a bit scared, I suppose. Several of the servants have heard . . . noises behind that door."

"A cat," I said. "Meowing."

"A cat." She nodded. "Many a person has heard it. I was told long ago, when I was a child, that the room's been locked since the eighteen hundreds. I don't know if it's true or not. I've never seen it open, that's for sure."

A cat key, I said to myself, *the key to a room where people heard a cat meowing.*

Inspector Bedford was inspecting the door all around its edges. "Well, if the key fits this room, it certainly hasn't been actually *used*. The paint is layers thick; it's sealed the whole door around. Has anyone got a knife?"

Dad went briefly into our rooms and came back with a sharp, thick knife.

"This might work," he said. He struggled and gouged until his knife had scored a clean pattern through the paint around the gaps of the door. It took a long time.

"Phew! That was tough!" he said. "But we're though the actual paint, I think."

Inspector Bedford inserted the key into the lock and struggled with it for ages. Dad had to fetch an oilcan in the end, and they oiled the lock. Finally the old key turned.

The door opened suddenly. A billow of thick dust came out.

"It's too dark to see!" Metcalf coughed. He was groping along the wall just inside the door. "I don't think there's a light switch in here."

"Wait," I said. "I'll get my flashlight." For some reason, I desperately wanted to go into that room first.

I ran for my flashlight. When I brought it back, they let me lead the way. Lord Minerva and Montague brought up the rear.

The flashlight lit up the curve of some mustard-colored drapes. They weren't window drapes, I saw, but bed drapes. The window drapes were crimson.

We were looking at a moth-eaten, cobwebbed four-poster bed. Its counterpane was covered in a thick layer of dust.

In fact, every surface was thick with dust. It billowed into the air as we moved about.

Near the bed was a small chest of drawers. On top of this was a cushion that had been infested at some time by house mice. It was embroidered with a name. WHITE MAURICE. I remembered that glimpse of the boy I'd seen, walking to and fro behind this door, a white cat in his arms.

This was Oswald's room.

The inspector pulled open the window drapes, coughing in the dust. Daylight shot in and lit it all up. We stood there in silence, looking around.

Here was the porcelain washstand in which he used to wash himself. Here were the silver-backed brushes he used to brush his hair. The bristles were clogged now with webs and dead spiders.

Here was a shelf, with a row of small wooden carvings of cats. Next to these was his penknife. He must have carved these cat figures himself.

"What on earth is *that* doing here?" I heard Dad exclaim.

I turned around. Dad was moving the drapes aside, looking at something on the four-poster bed.

There in the middle of the moldy pillow was something that should not have been there at all. It just didn't fit.

It wasn't anything from Oswald's time; that was clear. It was made of black plastic, about seven inches by four.

It was a videotape.

We all stared down at it, bewildered. How could this have possibly got into a room that had been closed up for so many years? Yet there it was, crisp and new, with not a speck of dust on it.

At my side I heard Montague give the slightest of gasps. Lord Minerva stared at the tape as if his eyes simply couldn't believe what they saw.

"Is there another way into this room?" asked the inspector. "There must be. This can't have come through *that* door, that's for sure!"

He and Dad inspected every inch of the walls and floor, but there was no other way in.

"How completely . . . strange!" muttered Dad.

Inspector Bedford picked up the videotape and turned to Dad. I could see that along its spine was a date, written in small red writing.

"Is there anywhere we can watch this?" he asked Dad.

Dad nodded. "In Lord Minerva's private study. I can't be sure, but I suspect this is one of the security tapes he records of the whole estate. I'll take you there."

So *this* was the thing that had disappeared, that Minerva assumed I'd stolen, and that Montague had been searching for so urgently. One of the security tapes.

Everyone filed back out, eager to see the tape. I lingered a moment. Mrs. B. did too.

This was a room belonging to one of the children, left just as it had been for all these years. Oswald's room. All his things lay here, just as they always had, even his beloved cat's bed. At my elbow Mrs. B. spoke softly.

"Maybe his mother couldn't bear to dismantle it after he died," she said. "Maybe she left it like this so that it looked like at any moment he could just come walking back in."

She bent down and touched the moth-eaten pillow gently. "I would have felt the same," she said, "if I could have ever been blessed with a child."

I followed her downstairs.

In the study, Inspector Bedford held the tape up and nodded toward the impressive array of tape players.

"Let's see it then, shall we?" he said. "Perhaps, Montague, you can assist us?"

It was hard to see who looked worse: Lord Minerva or his

butler. But Montague had no choice. He took the tape from the police inspector and slid it into the nearest console.

Lights lit up the screens. Then, on every screen, some images began to grow clearer.

First we saw the lake in flickering monochrome. The wind ruffled the surface of the water, and for a while this was all that could be seen. Then, off to one side, it became clear that people were moving.

On the little jetty two figures appeared. One stood taller than the other, who sat in some sort of chair. They were busy in the shadows.

Bending low, they were turning some small but obviously heavy bulk between them. The wind blew, and then the moon, waning, appeared above the clouds. It lit their work clearly, and I saw the glint of metal.

It was a chain.

The two men were finding the thing between them hard to wield, to move along the small jetty. Their faces became clear, moonlit.

It was Montague and Lord Minerva. Slowly they heaved that still form into the rowboat. Then Montague climbed uneasily into the boat beside it. Leaving Lord Minerva on the bank, he rowed the boat outward, right to the very middle of the lake. The boat lay so low in the water, so weighed down by its heavy load, that he had to row carefully, stealthily. Then he shipped his oars and reached for the bundle.

The small, chained figure of Einstein was lifted in the moonlight. It balanced, poised for a moment, on the rim of the boat. Then it vanished under the waves.

Inspector Bedford spoke briefly into his radio and then turned toward Minerva. "Lord Louis Minerva," he said," I am arresting you on suspicion of the murder of Lord Henry Minerva. . . ."

As his voice went on, I felt a strange emptying feeling. It was as if something that I had been carrying was suddenly seeping away, as if something heavy and dark were leaving me.

My legs went weak. I sagged against Dad.

It was over at last.

CHAPTER EIGHTEEN

WITHIN THE HOUR HIS nibs and Montague had been taken away to be interrogated. We went back up to our rooms: I and Dad and Sal and Mrs. B. She said hang the kitchen, the kitchen maids could handle it all, and she didn't care if they burned that old man's mansion right to the floor.

"Not with us in it, though," Sal said.

Then Dad and Sal kept wondering aloud how on earth the security tape had been placed inside the locked room.

"I mean, who left it?" asked Dad. "How did they get in? You all saw how it was sealed over with more than a hundred years of paint!"

"And there wasn't another way in," said Sal. "It's impossible! I mean, that tape just shouldn't have *been there*. Can you explain it, Jim?"

I shook my head. I thought I could explain it, but I was just too sad about Einstein to speak. I could imagine him going into his father's study and counting his way through all the security tapes until he found the right one, the one that showed his own death. He had been really clever about it all—a genius, in fact. He had let me think he was in danger when in fact he was already dead.

"This one, he likes cats," he had once told me out of the blue.

He had used what he could, to bring the whole thing to an end. He had hidden the security tape in the one place it was impossible for it to be, in the last place Minerva or Montague would think of looking—a room that was sealed up. He had known that between us, Mrs. B. and I would piece it together that the cat key must lead there. And locked doors were no barrier to Einstein—not by then.

Eventually, Inspector Bedford came and told us what he could. He looked down at Mrs. B. with sympathy in his eyes. "They drugged Henry," he said.

"Drugged him?" Mrs. B. gasped.

"The butler is confessing everything. Apparently, Minerva never loved Henry. He despised him, said he was an idiot."

Mrs. B. closed her eyes. "It's true. He never loved him. Poor little boy."

The inspector spoke again. "As for the school, we called them too. They'd received a phone call from Minerva, followed by a letter of confirmation. It said that Henry was to be home tutored from now on and wouldn't be returning to school. So they never even missed him."

"How did they drug him?" asked Sal.

"His bedtime cocoa."

Mrs. B. gave a small moan. "His cocoa?" she cried. "But I made it myself and sent it up to the south tower every night!"

"I'm so sorry, Mrs. Benson. They took it from the dumb-waiter and drugged it with Minerva's sleeping pills. As for the rest, well, you all saw it for yourself."

When at last evening fell and the sun went down and the moon came up, Mrs. B. sat alone in the small side kitchen and sobbed into her apron for a long time. Dad stood guard over her at the doorway, refusing to let anyone in to bother her.

"I know how it feels," he said simply.

Meanwhile, Sal and I sat on the bench outside the door. Sal asked me a million questions, but in the end Dad nudged her shoulder and shook his head. She finally went quiet and left me to my own thoughts. She looked pretty shaken up herself after everything she'd seen on the tape. But all I could think of was that my funny, strange friend was dead.

By the time we arrived here and I first saw him going into the maze, he'd already been dead for several days, murdered by his father. All because he was different from other people.

But just what exactly had he said to me about playing

truant? "This one, he did not go back to the school. This one, he does not like that school."

Einstein had spoken nothing but the truth. He'd never said he was skipping school at all. I'd just assumed he had. I'd assumed so much about this whole thing.

Later that night Dad insisted we all get in the car and go to the village, to get us out of Minerva for a while. He was driving Mrs. B. home for the night anyway and suggested we drop in on Eve and Jacob first. They had heard all about it and had telephoned to ask how I was.

Eve made a big fuss of us, with tea and coffee, cakes and cookies.

"Did you know him well?" Sal asked Eve. "Lord Henry?"

She shook her head. "Not really. I don't think anyone could claim to have known Henry *well*. Of us all, I suppose Alicia here knew him best. He didn't seem to dislike me exactly, but . . . well, when I tried to talk to him, he just kept walking away."

That figured.

Eve turned to Jacob. "You knew him a bit, though, didn't you, Dad?"

Jacob's medicine was obviously working. He replied quite calmly and normally. "Yes, I knew him. He used to walk down to the village sometimes. One minute I was alone, just walking the dogs, and the next minute there he was, plodding along next to me. He liked the dogs. He liked their names. 'Two dogs,' he said to me once. 'Two dogs, they have one name. P-H-I-G-H-D-O-U-G-H.' He liked things like that."

I nodded, smiling. Then they all stared at me (they kept doing that!), but I didn't want to tell them much. Not yet. They didn't press me.

Jacob walked to the window. "It's a good thing the lake's gone now. It was unlucky water. It drowned one of our ancestors long ago. She was an important woman. A cunning woman."

"Blind Meg," I said.

"Blind Meg. I've watched three children die suddenly at Minerva. Three in my own lifetime."

Everyone was quiet, listening to him.

"Edwina Minerva, 1916. I was only eight years old myself then. It had a big impact on my parents. I'll never forget them talking about it. I used to listen through the banisters."

"And then . . . Thomas?" I asked.

"Thomas Minerva. 1946," he replied. "He was a sickly boy; he had fits, sometimes several a week. He couldn't stand any excitement at all, no loud noises; everything seemed to trigger his fits."

I thought of the bells that had rung and killed him. Jacob gave a sigh.

"And then Beatrice, 1976. She was a sweet little thing,

260

always trying something new. People told her never to swim in the lake, but she was a bit of an adventurer, Beatrice. It was tragic."

We sipped at our tea or just sat silently. No one wanted to interrupt this new, lucid Jacob.

"It was always on the solstice that it happened," he went on in a soft voice. "It had happened before. My grandmother knew her history. She taught me how to make the old solstice crowns that used to be left at the seven stones. She said that the willow was a generous sort of spirit; after all, she let them take her green fingers so they could weave it into crowns. She let them weave her hair into all kinds of shapes, quite happily—as long as she was never uprooted. The roots of the willow must never be uprooted or damaged."

"But then the willow *was* damaged," I said, "when Lord Bartholomew made his lake."

He nodded. "They were just simple village folk, but the willow, she was everything to them. Her and the moon."

He stared up at the sky. The moonlight peeped down between the clouds and lit his face with silver. He seemed to have been growing in stature as he spoke. Eve looked mesmerized.

"Dad, I've never heard you talk like this," she said softly. "Why did you never tell all this to me when I was growing up?"

"Oh, Willow Evelyn!" he replied with a small laugh. "Have

you forgotten so soon? When you were very young, you thought you knew everything! Long before you were married and widowed, you would have nothing to do with the old local traditions. You grew to like gardening in the end, but when you were young, you despised it all. You thought you had nothing to learn from us. So how could we ever tell you?"

"Well, I'm listening now," she said quietly.

From the corner of my eye I saw Dad give a small smile. He knew this story well. His parents had wanted him to go into medicine—like them. But he didn't share their interests. His interest was in things he could grow with his own hands. Flowers and herbs and shrubs and trees. He too had been labeled "stubborn."

Abruptly Jacob's state of mind changed. He stared at the teapot longingly. "Any more tea in that pot?" he asked, beaming and rubbing his hands together. There was something in the way he said it that made us all laugh.

As more tea was poured and handed around, I thought of Einstein and his strange interests, his love of numbers, his obsession with them. I thought of his father's hatred of him, and a big lump came into my throat. But then I came to a decision as important as any I've ever made. I reached out and grabbed Dad's hand.

It was time to step away from loss.

* * *

Later, just as I climbed thankfully into bed, Dad came in with a strange look on his face.

"I've just had a call from Inspector Bedford," he said. "Lord Minerva has had a stroke. He got more and more angry at being arrested, and then, finally, he slumped to one side and had a massive stroke. He's completely paralyzed, can only move his eyes. I can't say I feel sorry for him, killing his son like he did."

He gave me an enormous hug good night and left the room.

I thought of Lord Louis Minerva III, sitting as still as one of his statues, trapped in his own body, just as Einstein had been trapped by his chains.

Dad decided to ignore his letter of dismissal from Lord Minerva. He continued being Head Gardener, and when English Heritage eventually brought Minerva Hall, they kept him on. So Sal and I could still wander around the huge grounds.

Einstein's remains were buried in Minerva's small chapel graveyard. We had to wait until the forensic work and the archaeologists were finished. We all went to the funeral, filing our way under the domed ceiling with the sun and moon and the stars all out at once.

His coffin was heaped in meadowsweet and willow. Outside, at my insistence, we lit a candle for each child and set it on their gravestones. Seven candles. Blind Meg had said:

When the seventh child walks with the six
And seven flames burn seven wicks,

then that would be the beginning of the end of all the misery.

And it was the same night of Einstein's funeral that—just after dusk—I went alone back down to the stone circle.

As I made my way there, I felt strangely excited. It was as if every dark thing that had happened since we'd arrived at Minerva were lifting. There was a new lightness in the air, a freshness. I'd been down to the village earlier that day and cut some willow boughs from the willow tree in Eve's garden. These I'd fashioned into a rough circlet.

It was peaceful and quiet by the stone circle. A few small shoots of weeds and grass were already beginning to show in the muddied ground. Life was taking over again in that place of death.

The seven sacred springs, hidden and buried so long ago, were showing signs of returning to their old courses. Maybe they would even once again join up and become one. Already the waterway that had caused flooding in the village every rainfall had dwindled back to the small, clear stream it once had been. I thought of all this as I walked to the central altar stone and laid the willow circlet on it.

I looked up and spotted a small figure, standing off to one side.

It was Einstein.

He stood alone and regarded his boots shyly, the boots that Mrs. B. had changed the laces of, to his favorite color, crayon blue. He still wouldn't look at me. But I knew he was well aware of me. I got the distinct feeling that he had come to say good-bye.

As I stared at him, I thought I saw something else, moving up by the gatehouse. It was just a shadow, a shimmer in the cool night air.

No. Not one shadow, I realized. *Six* shadows.

They clustered together at the start of the long lavender beds that stretched from the gatehouse.

There was absolutely no breeze at all, yet the lavender heads, right at the far end of the bed, bent and swayed strangely. It was as if unseen hands were running through them as the children walked back toward the chapel. Along the length of the lavender beds those lavender stalks bent and swayed, showing me where the children were—until finally they all went still. The air was filled with the thick, sweet scent of lavender.

The six children were going back to the place they had come from, the place they'd been laid to rest. I had the feeling that I wouldn't see any of them again. I watched them walk away, one by one.

Harriet, with her crimson dress with the big sleeves.

Oswald, with his blue silk suit and blond locks.

Little Nellie.

Edwina, the dancer.

Thomas, who had suffered from epilepsy.

And finally Beatrice, the adventurer, with her strong, brave face.

I looked back to where Einstein stood. I saw that he was pleased to see the children go. And I realized that he was as autistic in death as he had been in life. He wouldn't *want* to be with the children. He'd never wanted to be with them, to talk to them, to play with them. He had only liked animals. As soon as the children ever came close, he had always run away.

I knew he would stay here alone.

He stood there and wouldn't quite look at me. Nothing new there! A peacock cried out then, its haunting sound echoing over the garden of statues.

Then Einstein turned and walked away with his strange, plodding walk. As he did, a small white figure darted out of the bushes and began to follow him.

It was White Maurice, Oswald's cat.

Off they went together toward the maze, until they merged with the shadows of the dusk that was falling peacefully over the garden.

The whole place felt calm now, as if it could truly rest, as if it could thrive. As if summer had come.

EPILOGUE

I T WAS NOT QUITE TWO years later, on a hot, sunny evening, that we all sat chattering in the back garden of Eve's cottage.

It was Eve's birthday. Dad had helped Jacob organize this party for her. Most of the villagers had come to wish Eve well, but their real intention was to get together and organize the solstice festival, several weeks away and creeping ever closer.

The old custom of the Bringing of the Light had been resurrected, and everyone decided to do it every year, not just every thirty years. Even as they sat there discussing it, most of the adults were weaving willow circlets or trimming candles or cleaning old lanterns.

All around, the scattered remains of a picnic lay strewn: sandwiches, and scores of Mrs. B.'s pastries, and the hot-water pork pies that Sal had proudly made.

His nibs had died the year before in the prison hospital, having never recovered from his stroke. I wish I could have felt sorry for him, but I couldn't. As for Montague, he was still in prison, and would be for a very long time. Minerva Hall now belonged to the English Heritage, a historical trust that would preserve it as it was forever.

Three weeks from now our first summer solstice parade was going to take place in the grounds, by the Topiary Garden. From there it would be an easy journey toward the stone circle, for the Bringing of the Light ceremony.

Sal and I sat with our feet dangling above the old stream. We were idly plucking flowers of meadowsweet and chucking them down into the water. This water had indeed returned to the same place it used to emerge. There, torn from Eve's front room and restored, was the ancient culvert stone, the stream gurgling out of its dark mouth.

"Don't you mind ripping it out?" we'd all asked her.

"Mind? Why on earth should I mind? It belongs there, not in my house, not now the water's back to the way it should be."

We all had stared at the awful gap above the fireplace in her parlor.

"It's a mess!" said Sal.

"Oh, well, I'll just—oh, I don't know . . . have another fire-place built or something."

And Dad had offered to build it.

So one way or another we spent a lot of time down here.

Now I kicked off my shoes and stuck my toes into the water. It was crystal clear. Up at Minerva, the willow beds were growing back all along its path, and the banks of meadowsweet were returning.

Sal and I sat swatting at midges and chatting about nothing much. Then she told me off for shredding a dock leaf into smithereens.

"Must you always behave like some kind of crazed rodent at nesting time?" she snapped.

"Oh, shut up," I replied. "I'd rather be a rodent than a catty thing like you."

"Cats eat rodents," she said smugly.

I was just about to throw the shredded leaves at her when I saw her frown. She shielded her eyes from the sun and looked around, as if puzzled.

"What is it?" I asked.

She shook her head. "I . . . don't know. Something just . . . changed."

She got down from the bank until she stood on the pebbles of the streamside. She was staring at the dark mouth of the stream culvert. A new look came to her face: one of anticipation and growing excitement.

"Sal? What *is* it?"

"Shh!" she whispered. "Something's coming."

She bent toward the culvert mouth and stared down at it intently. And when I looked up, there stood Blind Meg on the opposite bank. I almost jumped out of my skin.

Her white hair was just as wild as ever, her back just as old and bent, her eyes just as closed and blind. But I could see that like Sal's, her whole attention was focused on the water that came tumbling out of the culvert, sparkling in the evening sun. It was as if she were listening for something, waiting for something important.

I watched her hand rise slowly until it pointed at the dark mouth of the culvert. Mesmerized, I watched Sal's hands get closer and closer to the culvert, as if she were trying to catch the water in her fingers. Then something small and round fell into Sal's cupped hand.

She dried it on her sweater. Her face grew incredulous as she stared down at it.

"What's that you've got there, Sal?" asked Eve as she walked up, followed by Dad and Jacob, Mrs. B., and both the Phighdoughs. On the opposite bank, Blind Meg's wrinkled old face became peaceful. She turned and walked away, fading from my sight until all I was looking at were the gentle fronds of willow drooping down.

Sal clambered back up the bank and held out something small in her palm toward Eve. "Look! " she whispered.

Eve picked it up. It was about one inch across. It was a

small stone carving of a willow crown.

It was roughly carved, the simple image of something that had been held sacred in this village for many centuries. It looked ancient. There were seven willow leaves, roughly interlaced.

"Is—is it what I think it is?" Sal asked in a wobbly voice.

Eve turned it over in her hands and nodded. "It's Blind Meg's healing charm! It must be," she said, sounding awed.

I remembered that the night she drowned, the cunning woman had been planning to pass this badge of office on. It had been lost in the mud of Minerva for all this time, ever since the greedy Lord Bartholomew had flooded the valley to make his carp lake.

"Where on earth did you *find* it?" asked Eve.

Sal pointed. "There! Just there at the culvert. I caught it as it came out!"

Eve looked up the road toward Minerva. We all did. In our mind's eye, we were tracing this underground watercourse all the way back to Minerva.

"It must have been washed downhill after the lake was drained and the waterways altered!" Dad said. "It must have been making its way down here for two whole years!"

Jacob's face lit up as he reached for it. "It's nice!" he said. "Can I eat it?"

Eve snatched it away, and Dad handed him a half-eaten

cookie instead. He munched at it, perfectly content.

Eve held the ancient talisman out toward Sal. "Take it," she said.

But Sal shook her head. "It's yours first," she said. "It belongs to your family, to all those healing women through the centuries. Besides, it's *your* birthday!"

"But you found it!" said Eve. "And there's another thing too . . . your name."

Sal frowned. "My name?"

Eve nodded. "In the medieval Celtic, the name of the willow is *saille*. This has been anglicized to Sally. It means 'one who comes forth, as supple as the willow.' So you see, Sal, it's not just me that's named after the Willow. It's you."

Sal looked suddenly radiant as they stared across at each other.

"Take it," Eve repeated to Sal, still holding the charm out. "You found it."

"No," said Sally quietly. "*It* found *you*. It's not for me. Not yet."

I got the feeling suddenly that Sal knew something I didn't know. They exchanged a long, shrewd glance until Eve finally nodded.

"All right," said Eve. "It'll belong to you one day anyway, eventually."

Sal took Dad by one hand and Jacob by the other. "Come

on," she said to Dad. "Let's go make another willow crown. I'm getting better at them. As for you, Jacob, it's time for your Rubik's Cube. Now, where on earth did you put it?"

Jacob beamed. "I ate it!" he declared happily.

I sat there by myself, listening to their background chatter, long after they'd all moved away. At my feet gurgled the ancient stream from Minerva; the seven springs, united again. As darkness began to fall, I thought of Blind Meg, who had come back to Culvert Cottage for one last time. This had been her garden too, her stream. She had probably sat here once, just like me, wrapped up in the scent of meadowsweet. She had foreseen all this with those old, sightless eyes.

I thought of those people from long ago, our ancestors, who worked in bronze and early iron, who worshiped the sun and the moon and who lived in harmony with the ancient spirits of nature. I thought of everything that had happened, of the chain of events that had been unfolding for all those centuries, to restore the land back to the old spirits.

*SO YOUNG AND OLD CAN COME TO GREET
THE WILLOW FAIR THE MEADOWSWEET*

ACKNOWLEDGMENTS

To be honest, whenever I've read in the past the way some writers wax lyrical in their thanks, I've wondered at the need for quite such a profusion of gratitude.

Now I get it.

So I can say unreservedly that this novel would not and could not have been written without Katherine Tegen. Her patience and understanding were above and beyond the call of duty—and in reading this, you are not hearing the half of it.

The same must be said of her assistant, Emily Lawrence, whose cheery emails and strong advice made a difference.

As to my agent, Eunice McMullen, she has needed immense patience, stamina, and tact, and supplied it.

Thank you so much, all three.

On the Home Front, no one who has an inkling of my true

nature and weird working practices can understand how my husband, Greg, puts up with it all. To elaborate would begin to sound trite and twee . . . thankfully, he is good at reading between the lines.

To my children:

Thanks go to Robin. You have been a splendid helper and enhancer of all this, and your perseverance became something I could lean on.

To Wyl. You have been gracious even when I haven't. Enough said.

To Alex and Noni, for care, support, and fun.

Thanks go to my mother, Catherine, and my sisters, Anne and Jan, for being part of the bigger story. Also to Frank and Sue, whose visit spurred me on at a particularly weary moment. Thanks for coming all that way. It was good to see you both. It was time.

To Anna Palliser, for sudden magic, batiks, and bursts of sherbet to a jaded palate. To her daughter Seren—for physically lifting the Amazon stone and bringing me that image.

Thanks and "dings" go to Janet Graniola, for sending sugar and spice and all things nice . . . and for widdershinning merrily away with me.

To Theseus, for your read-throughs, and for joining me in hearing pterodactyls on the conservatory roof, instead of sparrows.

Thanks once again to my friends (including hosts) at the Highcliffe Hotel, Sheffield—especially all members of my poker team. Bai gum! There's nothing quite like a competitive game of Texas Hold 'Em to make you forget the problems of syntax, character, and plot!

To Chris Burdett—me old mucker!—and to Nick, for all the uplifting banter and insults on quiz night.

To Sian, for always being sweet to me, no matter what. To Helen for the laughs. People sometimes don't realize what a difference they make to others. To John, who keeps his signed copy of *The Riddles of Epsilon* in a cellophane wrapper—pristine—from Christine. I promised you the very first copy of *The Hunt for the Seventh*. I meant it.

Gratitude also to my strange and colorful friends Nia Arongowarra, Jon Brightplace, Pacos, and "Have-A-Go Jack."

Finally, thanks go to someone who has known me only for three years and yet has become supportive and interested in the extreme. He has been at various times editor, teacher, blunt advisor, friend, copy reader, new-family-member and creative touchstone.

If I could buy you your very own Starbucks, Nathan Brown—I would. You certainly deserve it.

Love to you all,

Christine